# Morien

D1732994

## By
## Jessie Laidlay Weston

ANODOS
BOOKS

Jessie Laidlay Weston (1850-1928)
Originally published in 1901.

Anodos Books
1c Kings Road
Whithorn
Newton Stewart
Dumfries & Galloway
DG8 8PP

# Contents

# PREFACE

The metrical romance of which the following pages offer a prose translation is contained in the mediæval Dutch version of the *Lancelot*, where it occupies upwards of five thousand lines, forming the conclusion of the first existing volume of that compilation. So far as our present knowledge extends, it is found nowhere else.

Nor do we know the date of the original poem, or the name of the author. The Dutch MS. is of the commencement of the fourteenth century, and appears to represent a compilation similar to that with which Sir Thomas Malory has made us familiar, *i.e.*, a condensed rendering of a number of Arthurian romances which in their original form were independent of each other. Thus, in the Dutch *Lancelot* we have not only the latter portion of the *Lancelot* proper, the *Queste*, and the *Morte Arthur*, the ordinary component parts of the prose *Lancelot* in its most fully developed form, but also a portion of a *Perceval* romance, having for its basis a version near akin to, if not identical with, the poem of Chrétien de Troyes, and a group of episodic romances, some of considerable length, the majority of which have not yet been discovered elsewhere.[1]

Unfortunately, the first volume of this compilation, which was originally in four parts, has been lost; consequently we are without any of the indications, so often to be found in the opening lines of similar compositions, as to the personality of the compiler, or the material at his disposal; but judging from those sections in which comparison is possible, the *Lancelot*, *Queste*, and *Morte Arthur*, the entire work is a translation, and a very faithful translation, of a French original. It is quite clear that the Dutch compiler understood his text well, and though possibly somewhat hampered by the necessity of turning prose into verse (this version, contrary to the otherwise invariable rule of the later *Lancelot* romances, being rhymed), he renders it with remarkable fidelity. The natural inference, and that drawn by M. Gaston Paris, who, so far, appears to be the only scholar who has seriously occupied himself with this interesting version, is that those

---

[1] *Cf.* my *Legend of Sir Lancelot du Lac*; Grimm Library, vol. xii., chapter ix., where a brief summary of the contents of the Dutch *Lancelot* is given.

episodic romances, of which we possess no other copy, are also derived from a French source. Most probably, so far as these shorter romances are concerned, the originals would be metrical, not prose versions, as in the case of the *Lancelot* sections.

It is true that with regard to the romance here translated, *Morien*, the Dutch scholars responsible for the two editions in which it has appeared, MM. Jonckbloet and Te Winkel, the former the editor of the whole compilation, the latter of this section only, are both inclined to regard the poem as an original Dutch composition; but M. Gaston Paris, in his summary of the romance (*Histoire Litteraire*, vol. xxx. p. 247) rejects this theory as based on inadequate grounds. It must be admitted that an original Arthurian romance of the twelfth or thirteenth century, when at latest such a poem would be written, in a language other than French, is so far unknown to us; and although as a matter of fact the central *motif* of the poem, the representation of a Moor as near akin to the Grail Winner, Sir Perceval, has not been preserved in any known French text, while it does exist in a famous German version, I for one find no difficulty in believing that the tradition existed in French, and that the original version of our poem was a metrical romance in that tongue.

So far as the story of *Morien* is concerned, the form is probably later than the tradition it embodies. In its present shape it is certainly posterior to the appearance of the Galahad *Queste*, to which it contains several direct references; such are the hermit's allusion to the predicted circumstances of his death, which are related in full in the *Queste*; the prophecy that Perceval shall "aid" in the winning of the Holy Grail, a quest of which in the earlier version he is sole achiever; and the explicit statements of the closing lines as to Galahad's arrival at Court, his filling the Siege Perilous, and achieving the Adventures of the Round Table. As the romance now stands it is an introduction to the *Queste*, with which volume iii. (volume ii. of the extant version) of the Dutch *Lancelot* opens.

But the opening lines of the present version show clearly that in one important point, at least, the story has undergone a radical modification. Was it the Dutch translator or his source who substituted Agloval, Perceval's brother, for the tradition which made Perceval himself the father of the hero? M. Gaston Paris takes the former view; but I am inclined to think that the alteration was already in the French source. The Grail of Sir Agloval's vision is the Grail of Castle Corbenic and the *Queste*; unless we are to consider this vision as the addition of the Dutch compiler (who, when we are in a position to test his work does not interpolate such additions), we must, I think, admit that the romance in the form in which it reached him was already at a stage in which Perceval could not, without violence to the then existing conception of his character, be considered as the father, or the brother, of Morien. To reconstruct the original story it would be necessary not merely to eliminate all mention of Agloval, as suggested by M. Gaston Paris, but the Grail references would also require modification. As it stands, the poem is a curious mixture of conflicting traditions.

In this connection it appears to me that the evidence of the *Parzival* is of primary importance; the circumstances attending the birth of Feirefis are exactly parallel with those of Morien—in both a Christian knight wins the love of a Moorish princess; in both he leaves her before the birth of her son, in the one case with a direct, in the other with a conditional, promise to return, which promise is in neither instance kept; in both the lad, when grown to manhood, sets out to seek his father; in both he apparently makes a practice of fighting with every one whom he meets; in the one version he is brother, in the other son or nephew, to Perceval. The points of difference are that whereas Morien is black all over, save his teeth, Feirefis is parti-coloured, black and white—a curious conception, which seems to point to an earlier stage of thought; Morien is a Christian, Feirefis a heathen—the more probable version.

It is easy to understand why the hero ceased to be considered Perceval's son—the opening lines of the poem describe the situation perfectly; but I do not think it has been sufficiently realised that precisely the same causes which would operate to the suppression of this relationship would equally operate to the suppression of that of the *Parzival*. Perceval, the virgin winner of the Grail, could not have a *liaison* with a Moorish princess, but neither could Perceval's father, the direct descendant of Joseph of Arimathea, and hereditary holder of the Grail. The *Early History*

3

of that talisman, as related by Robert de Borron, once generally accepted, the relationship of *brother* was as impossible as that of *son*.

It seems clear that if a genuine tradition of a Moor as near kinsman to Perceval really existed—and I see no reason to doubt that it did—it must have belonged to the Perceval story prior to the development of the Grail tradition, *e.g.*, to such a stage as that hinted at by the chess-board adventure of the "Didot" *Perceval* and Gautier's poem, when the hero was as ready to take advantage of his *bonnes fortunes* as other heroes of popular folk tales.

Further, judging from these stories it would seem probable that the requisite modification began with the earlier generation, *i.e.*, Perceval himself still retaining traces of his secular and folk-tale origin, while his father and mother have already been brought under the influence of the ecclesiasticised Grail tradition. That this would be the case appears only probable when we recall the vague and conflicting traditions as to the hero's parentage; it was Perceval himself, and not his father or his mother, who was the important factor in the tale; hence the change in his character was a matter of gradual evolution. Thus I am of opinion that the Moor as Perceval's brother is likely to be an earlier conception than the Moor as Perceval's son. It is, I think, noticeable that the romance containing this feature, the *Parzival*, also, contrary to the *Early History* versions, connects him with the Grail through his mother, instead of through his father.

The *Morien* is for me a welcome piece of evidence in support of the theory that sees in the poem of Wolfram von Eschenbach the survival of a genuine variant of the *Perceval* story, differing in important particulars from that preserved by Chrétien de Troyes, and based upon a French original, now, unfortunately, lost.

For this, if for no other reason, the poem would, it seems to me, be worth introducing to a wider circle of readers than that to which in its present form it can appeal. The students of old Dutch are few in number, and the bewildering extent of the *Lancelot* compilation, amounting as it does, even in its incomplete state, to upwards of 90,000 lines, is sufficient in itself to deter many from its examination. *Morien* in its original form is, and can be, known to but few. But not only does it represent a tradition curious and interesting in itself, it has other claims to attention; even in a translation it is by no means ill written; it is simple, direct, and the adventures are not drawn out to wearisome length by the introduction of unnecessary details. The characterisation too, is good; the hero is well realised, and Gawain, in particular, appears in a most favourable light, one far more in accordance with the earlier than with the later stage of Arthurian tradition; the contrast between his courteous self-restraint and the impetuous ardour of the young savage is well conceived, and the manner in which he and Gareth contrive to check and manage the turbulent youth without giving him cause for offence is very cleverly indicated. Lancelot is a much more shadowy personage; if, as suggested above, the original story took shape at a period before he had attained to his full popularity, and references to his valour were added later we can understand this. It is noticeable that the adventure assigned to him is much less original in character, and told with far less detail than that ascribed to Gawain.

The romance as we have it presents, as remarked before, a curious mixture of earlier and later elements. None of the adventures it relates are preserved in any English text. Alike as a representative of a lost tradition, and for its own intrinsic merit it has seemed to me, though perhaps inferior in literary charm to the romances previously published in this series, to be yet not unworthy of inclusion among them.

BOURNEMOUTH, *July* 1901

# MORIEN

Herein *doth the adventure tell of a knight who was named Morien. Some of the books give us to wit that he was Perceval's son, and some say that he was son to Agloval, who was Perceval's brother, so that he was nephew unto that good knight. Now we find it written for a truth that Perceval and Galahad alike died virgin knights in the quest of the Holy Grail; and for that cause I say of Perceval that in sooth he was not Morien's father, but that rather was Morien his brother's son. And of a Moorish princess was he begotten at that time when Agloval sought far and wide for Lancelot, who was lost, as ye have read here afore.*

*I ween that he who made the tale of Lancelot and set it in rhyme forgot, and was heedless of, the fair adventure of Morien. I marvel much that they who were skilled in verse and the making of rhymes did not bring the story to its rightful ending.*

Now as at this time King Arthur abode in Britain, and held high court, that his fame might wax the greater; and as the noble folk sat at the board and ate, there came riding a knight; for 'twas the custom in Arthur's days that while the king held court no door, small nor great, should be shut, but all men were free to come and go as they willed.

Thus the knight came riding where the high folk sat, and would fain have dismounted, but so sorely was he wounded that he might not do so. In sooth he was in evil case, for he had more than ten wounds, and from the least of them a man might scarce recover; he came in such guise that his weapons and his vesture and his steed, which was fair and tall, were all dyed red with his own blood. The knight was sad at heart and sorely wounded, yet he greeted, as best he might, all the lords then in the hall; but more he might not speak, for the pain of his wounds.

Then my lord, Sir Gawain, who did full many a courtesy (for such was his wont all his life long), so soon as he saw the knight, sprang up with no delay, and lifted him from the saddle and set him upon the ground, but he might neither sit, nor walk, nor so much as stand upon his feet, but fell upon the earth.

Then Sir Gawain bade them carry him softly on a couch to the side of the hall in the sight of the chief guests, that they might hear his tale. But since he might scarce speak he made him to be disarmed, and stripped to the skin, and wrapped in warm coverings and gave him a sop steeped in clear wine.

Then Sir Gawain began to search his wounds, for in those days, so far as God suffered the sun to shine might no man find one so skilled in leech-craft, for that man whom he took in his care, were the life but left in him, would neither lack healing nor die of any wound.

Then spake the knight who lay there: "Woe is me, for I may neither eat nor drink; my heart beginneth to sink, mine eyes fail me, methinks I am about to die! Yet might I live, and would God grant to me that all ye who sit here beside me might hear my words, I had fain spoken with the king, whom I sought as best I might, in that I would not be forsworn; needs must I come hither!"

Then quoth Sir Gawain the good: "Sir Knight, have ye no dread of death as at this time, for I shall help you to a respite." He drew forth from his pouch a root that had this virtue, that it stayed the flow of blood and strengthened the feeble; he placed it in the knight's mouth, and bade him eat a little; therewith was his heart lightened, and he began to eat and to drink, and forgat somewhat of his pain.

Erst when the service was ended came King Arthur to the knight as he lay, and said: "God give ye good-day, dear Sir Knight; tell me who hath wounded ye so sorely, and how came ye by your hurt? Did the knight who wrought such harm depart from ye unscathed?"

Then spake the knight to the king, who stood before him: "That will I tell ye, for I am sworn and pledged thereto. 'Tis seven years past that I lost all my goods, and poverty pressed me so sorely that I knew not what I might do. Thus would I keep myself by robbery. My tithes had I sold, I had spent all my goods, and pledged all my heritage, so that of all that my father left when he departed from this world there remained to me nothing. Naught, not a straw, had I left. Yet had I given much in largesse, for I had frequented many a tourney and Table Round where I had scattered my goods; whosoever craved aught of me, whether for want or for reward, were he page, were he messenger, never did he depart empty-handed. Never did I fail any who besought aid of me. Thus I spent all my goods. Then must I fare through the land; and did I meet folk (though at first I shamed me) whomsoever I met, whether pilgrim or merchant, did he bear goods or money with him, so did I deal with him that I won it for myself. But little might escape me. I have done many an evil deed! Now is it three days past since, as I fared on my way, a knight met me, and I deemed his steed so good that I coveted it above all things, but when I laid hands upon the bridle and bade the knight dismount then was he ready with his sword and repaid me with such a blow that I forgot who I was and all that had befallen me; so fierce was the stroke he dealt me! And though I betook me to arms they profited me not a jot; his blows were so heavy, they weighed even as lead. He pierced through my harness, as ye may see in many places, smiting through flesh and bone. But from me did he receive no blow that might turn to his loss. Therefore must I yield myself to him, and swear by my troth, would I save my life, to come hither to ye as swiftly as I might, and delay no whit, but yield me your prisoner. And this have I now done, and I yield myself to your grace, Sir King, avowing my misdeeds that I have wrought in this world, whether in thought or deed."

Then quoth the king: "Wit ye well who he was, and how he was hight, who sent ye hither? Of what fashion was his steed, and what tokens did he bear?"

And the knight answered: "Of that ye would ask me may I tell ye naught, save only that the knight's steed and armour were red as blood, and he seemed to me of Wales by his speech, and by all I might discern of him. Thereto is he of such might that I ween his equal may scarce be found in Christendom; that may I also say in truth, since such ill chance befell me that I met with him when my intent was evil, and not good."

Then King Arthur cried aloud that all might hear him, that the knight was surely none other than Sir Perceval. He tore his hair, and demeaned himself as one sorely vexed, and spake: "Though I be lord of riches yet may I say that I am friendless! This may I say forsooth; since I lost Perceval, and the ill chance befell me that he had the will and the desire to seek the Grail and the spear (which he may not find) many a wounded knight hath he sent as captive to my court, whom, for their misdoing, he hath vanquished by his might. Ever shall he be thanked therefor. Now have I no knight so valiant of mind that for my sake will seek Perceval and bring him to court. Yet I and my court and my country alike are shamed and dishonoured in that we have so long lacked his presence, and for this am I above measure sorrowful."

Then spake Sir Kay the seneschal: "God-wot I shall fetch Perceval, whether he will or no, and bring hither to court him whom ye praise so highly, and believe me well, were he wrought of iron, by the God who made me I will bring him living or dead! Does this content ye, my lord king?"

Then stood Arthur and laughed aloud, and likewise did all the knights who heard Sir Kay speak. And the king said: "Sir Kay, let this talk be; ye should of right be shamed when ye hear the Welshman's name! Have ye altogether forgot how ye boasted yourself aforetime, even as ye have now done, and then how ye met Perceval, whom ye had scarce sought? There were ye ill-counselled; ye thought to bring him without his will, but the knight was not so feeble, he gave ye a blow that brake your collar-bone and thrust ye from your steed, feet upward, with little honour! Had he so willed he had slain ye. Idle boasting is great shame. An I hear ye make further boast of seeking knights I shall owe ye small thanks. Little would he heed your compelling! In such quest must another ride would I be comforted by the coming of this knight!"

Quoth Sir Gawain, "Ye mind me of an old saying, Sir Kay, how if some men grow old, and God should spare them even to an hundred years, then would they be but the more foolish—such an one, methinks, are ye! Now believe ye my tale; did ye once find Perceval, an ye thought to say to him other than he chose to hear, by the Lord above us ye dare not do it for the king's crown, who is lord of this land, he would put ye to such great shame! Of long time, and full well, do I know his ways! When he is well entreated, and men do naught to vex him, then is he gentle as a lamb, but an ye rouse him to wrath then is he the fiercest wight of God's making—in such wise is he fashioned. Gentle and courteous is he to all the world, rich and poor, so long as men do him no wrong, but let his temper be changed, and nowhere shall ye find his fellow!"

After this manner also spake Sir Lancelot, and all who were in the hall took up the word of Sir Gawain, and praised Perceval. But there were many in the court heavy at heart, and sore vexed with the king their lord for that he held them so cheap.

Quoth the Father of Adventure, "By the might of our Lord, and by His name, who ruleth in heaven, henceforth I will not rest in one place more than one night or two, but will ride ever till I have found Perceval, or learnt certain tidings of his doings; and I will bring him to court an he be minded to ride with me—further will I not vaunt myself."

Then spake Arthur, "God wot, here have I both joy and sorrow. Fain am I to behold Perceval, an such fortune befall me, and ill may I spare thee. Thus have I joy and sorrow. Yet, nephew, trow me well, I were loth to bid thee break thine oath; now, therefore, make ready as befits thee, and depart as swiftly as may be, and seek me Perceval."

With these words up sprang Sir Lancelot of the Lake, and stepped forward, and spake, and said he would adventure himself and take what fortune should send, and go seek Perceval hither and thither through all lands; "And may I but find that proud knight, an it lieth in my power, hither will I bring him! Now will I make me ready, and ride hence without longer tarrying; methinks, from the king's word, an he have Perceval he shall be freed from care—so will I ride hence for his honour."

Quoth Arthur the king: "Sir Lancelot, of this thing it behoves ye take better rede; lightly might it turn to my shame if all my knights rode forth, and I thereafter were beset with strife and warfare, as full oft hath chanced aforetime! So might it in sooth be mine undoing. It hath chanced afore this that I had lost crown and lands, save for my knights; by them have I been victorious!"

Quoth Sir Lancelot: "By the Lord who made me, and who shall be Doom's-man at the last day, come what may thereof, since Sir Gawain rideth hence 'tis not I will bide behind! Rather will I try what may chance, and adventure all that God hath given me, for he sought me with all his power when I was in secret case, and brought me once more to court—for that do I owe him faith and fellowship."

Then they all wept, wives and maidens, knights and squires, when they knew Sir Lancelot would ride thence.

Sir Gawain, who forgat not the wounded knight and his need of healing, went to him as he lay, and bound up his wounds, and so tended him at that time that he was healed ere long—needs must he be healed, even against his will, on whom Sir Gawain laid hands. All they of the court were sad and sorry at their departing; that eve they ate but little, for thinking of the knights who should ride forth with the morning.

But now will we be silent on their lamentations, and tell

henceforth of Sir Gawain and Sir Lancelot, who rode both on their way.

The adventure doeth us to wit that in the morning, so soon as it was day, they rode forth together through many a waste land, over many a heath and high hill, adown many a valley to seek Sir Perceval, but little did it profit them, for of him might they learn naught. Thus were they sorely vexed.

On the ninth day there came riding towards them a knight on a goodly steed, and well armed withal. He was all black, even as I tell ye: his head, his body, and his hands were all black, saving only his teeth. His shield and his armour were even those of a Moor, and black as a raven. He rode his steed at full gallop, with many a forward bound. When he beheld the knights, and drew nigh to them, and the one had greeted the other, he cried aloud to Sir Lancelot: "Knight, now give me to wit of one thing which I desire, or guard ye against my spear. The truth will I know. I shall tell ye herewith my custom; what knight soever I may meet, were he stronger than five men, and I knew it well, yet would I not hold my hand for fear or favour, but he should answer me, or I should fight against him. Now, Sir Knight, give me answer, by your troth, so truly as ye know, to that which I shall ask ye, and delay not, otherwise may ye well rue it!"

Quoth Sir Lancelot: "I were liefer dead than that a knight should force me to do that to which I had no mind—so were the shame equal. Hold to your custom an ye will; I were more fain to fight than to let ye be, if but to fell your pride. I ask naught but peace, yet will I chastise your discourtesy, or die in that will!"

The Moor, who was wroth with Sir Lancelot, abode not still, but reined back his steed, and laid his spear in rest as one who was keen to fight. Sir Gawain drew on one side, since the twain would fight, and thought in himself, as was right and courteous, that it were folly, and the custom of no good knight, for twain to fall on one man, since life stood not at stake. 'Twere time enough for him to take hand therein, and stand by his comrade, did he see him hard pressed. Therefore stood Sir Gawain still, as one who had no mind to fight, nor to break the laws of courtesy. Nevertheless he deemed that this was a devil rather than a man whom they had come upon! Had they not heard him call upon God no man had dared face him, deeming that he was the devil or one of his fellows out of hell, for that his steed was so great, and he was taller even than Sir Lancelot, and black withal, as I said afore.

Thus came the two together, the Moor and Sir Lancelot; each had a great spear and brake it in two, as a reed, yet neither felled the other, but each abode upon his steed. Then each drew his sword from its sheath, and set to work therewith, and of a sooth, had not God Himself so willed it both had died there; so mighty were their strokes that by right no man should escape alive. Had it been midnight, and dark as night is wont to be, yet had ye seen the grass and the flowers by the light of the sparks that flew so thick from helmet and sword and fell upon the earth. The smith that wrought their weapons I say he wrought them not amiss, he merited a fairer reward than Arthur ever gave to any man for such desert.

The knight and Sir Lancelot, neither would yield to the other till Sir Gawain parted them by his prayer, and made them withdraw each from the other, for great pity he deemed it should either there be slain; yet so fell were the blows that they smote, and so great their wrath withal, that he saw well did the strife endure but short while longer they had received such wounds as should be the death of one, or it might well be of both.

When Sir Gawain had parted the twain, whom he saw to be weary enow, he spake to the Moor: "'Tis an ill custom this to which ye are given; ye shall here renounce it. Had ye but asked in courteous wise that which ye have a mind to know, this knight had hearkened, and had answered ye of right goodwill; he had not refused, that do I know well. Ye be both rash and foolish, and one of the twain, ye, or he, shall lose by it, and from that do I dissent, an ye show me not better reason therefore."

Quoth the Moor: "How come ye to speak thus to me? Wot ye that I be afraid to fight against the twain of ye; or that I have held my hand through fear of death? Were the one of ye Sir Lancelot, and the other King Arthur's sister's son (these twain are wont to be praised above all in Arthur's court as I have ofttimes heard, though never have I seen them), yet would I not yield a foot to them!"

Then thought Sir Gawain with himself, "We were foolish and unwise an we failed to show courtesy to one who praises us so highly."

But Sir Lancelot had great lust either to win the fight or to play it to a loss, and Sir Gawain, who was well ware of this, prayed him straitly, by the love he bare to him, and to King Arthur his lord, that for their honour he should hold his peace awhile, and let him say his will: "And this I charge ye, by the faith ye owe to my lady, my uncle's wife."

Sir Lancelot spake: "Of a sooth, an ye had not thus charged me I should have avenged myself or here been slain, in that this knight forced the strife upon me without cause, and loaded me with blows; but in that ye so conjure me, I am he that will harm no man for profit to myself save that he first attack me. And since it seemeth good to ye I will e'en lay the strife in respite. God grant me good counsel therein, since I do it not for cowardice, but for love of ye and for your prayer."

Thus stood the three in the open, and Sir Gawain spake to the Moor: "Ye be foolish in that ye do such things—now, neither we nor ye are harmed, yet might ye lightly do that which should cost ye your life. Tell me what ye seek, and I will give ye good counsel withal. If I may I shall tell ye that which ye should courteously have asked of this knight, who never yet was so hardly bestead by any man that he fell from his steed."

Quoth the Moor: "Ye say well. Now I pray ye by all who own the laws of knighthood, and by Sir Gawain afore all, since he is reckoned the best, he and Sir Lancelot, wherever it may be, in whatever need, far and wide throughout the world, of all men are these twain most praised (I myself know naught save that which I have heard tell), know ye aught of Sir Agloval, brother to Sir Perceval of Wales? Of him have I asked many, this long while past; I have ridden hither and thither this half year, and here and there have I sought him. For this have I dared many a peril, and here will I lie dead save that ye twain tell me, in friendship or in fight, if ye know aught of Sir Agloval. Now have we had enow of this talk; 'tis full time ye answer, or we take up our strife once again, and see the which of us hath the sooner his full."

Sir Gawain hearkened, and smiled at the black knight's speech, and spake soothfastly: "Now tell me what ye will of Sir Agloval that ye thus seek him, and thereafter will I tell ye that which I know."

And the Moor answered straightway: "So will I tell ye all. Sir Agloval is my father, 'twas he begat me. And more will I tell ye; it chanced aforetime as ye may now learn, when he came into the land of the Moors; there through his valiant deeds he won the heart of a maiden, she was my mother, by my troth. So far went the matter between them through their words and through his courtesy, and because he was so fair to look upon, that she gave him all his will—the which brought her small reward, and great sorrow. Each plighted their troth to the other ere she granted him her favours. Therein was she ill-counselled, for he forsook her thereafter—'tis more than fourteen years past; and when he parted from her she bare me, though he knew it not. He told her his quest, whereof he was sore troubled, and how it came about that he must needs leave her, and that will I now tell ye. My father was seeking a noble knight, who was lost as at that time, and who was hight Sir Lancelot. Still more may I tell ye; he told my mother that he and many of his fellows had sworn a great oath to seek Sir Lancelot, and their quest should endure two years or more an they found him not, or could learn no tidings of him. Nor should they tarry in any land more than one night or two. This vexed my father sorely, that for this cause, and to keep his oath, he must needs leave my mother. But ere he departed he sware to her that he would return when he had achieved his quest; but he kept not his oath. Thus have I sought him in many a court. All this did my lady mother tell me, and also of the troth-plight. Little good hath it done me that he be my father, and that he sware to my mother, ere he departed, that for her honour, and for her profit, he would return to her without fail. Doth he live, God send him mocking (this I pray in all humility), but an he be already dead, then may God forgive him his sins. I and my mother are disinherited, since that he hath deserted us, of great goods and of a fair heritage, that which fell to her from her father have we lost altogether. It hath been denied us by the law of the land. Thereto was I greatly shamed, for they called me fatherless, and I could shew naught against it, nor tell them who it was that begat me, since my father had thus fled. So did I cause myself to be dubbed knight, and sware a great oath (I were loth to break it) that never should I meet a knight but I would fight him, or he should tell me if he perchance knew any tidings of my father, that I might learn somewhat concerning him. Did I meet mine own brother, I would not break mine oath, nor my vow; and till now have I kept it well, nor broken it by my default. And here would I bid ye twain, if ye would part from me in friendship, that ye tell me what ye may know thereof, out and out, by your troth, and therewith end this talk. Otherwise let us end this matter even as we began it, for there liveth no knight under the sun for whom I would break mine oath, were it for my hurt, or for my profit."

Then was there neither of the twain, Sir Gawain nor Sir Lancelot, but the tears fell from their eyes when they heard the knight's tale. Such pity had they for him, they waxed pale, and red, and discovered their faces, when they heard his plaint.

Quoth Sir Lancelot: "By my good days, nevermore will I be wrathful, nor bear rancour against ye for any lack of courtesy; ye need no longer stand on guard against me, my heart is not evil towards ye, and we will counsel ye well."

Then was the black knight blithe, and drew near to Sir Lancelot, and bared his head, which was black as pitch; that was the fashion of his land—Moors are black as burnt brands. But in all that men would praise in a knight was he fair; after his kind. Though he were black, what was he the worse? In him was naught unsightly; he was taller by half a foot than any knight who stood beside him, and as yet was he scarce more than a child! It pleased him so well when he heard them speak thus of Sir Agloval that he knelt him straightway on the earth; but Sir Gawain raised him up, and told him their tidings, how they were but as messengers, and belonged to the court of King Arthur, which was of high renown, and that they rode at that time seeking Sir Perceval and Sir Agloval, since the king desired them both. "And his mind is to see and speak with them; may we by any means persuade those noble knights we shall return straightway to the king's court, an it be so that they will ride with us (further will we not vaunt ourselves, 'tis of our good will, and their pleasure), thereby shall the king be the more honoured. They belong to the Round Table, and have done so of long time; both are of the king's court, and knights of high renown. Now an ye will work wisely, and shun your own harm, ye will mount, and ride to King Arthur's court, and delay not. I hope in God that Sir Agloval shall come thither within short space, or that ye shall hear tidings of him; for there come full oft tidings from afar. Go ye to court without tarrying, the king will receive ye well. Tell him, and give him to wit who ye be, and whence ye come, and the quest upon which ye ride; he will not let ye depart ere we come and bring with us your father, an God prosper us. Should ye ride thus through the land, and fight with every knight whom ye may meet, ye will need great good fortune to win every conflict without mischance or ill-hap! They who will be ever fighting, and ne'er avoid a combat, an they hold such custom for long, though at whiles they escape, yet shall they find their master, who will perforce change their mood! Now Sir Knight do our bidding, for your own honour's sake, and ride ye to court; grant us this grace, for ere ye have abode long time there I hope that ye shall behold your father or receive tidings of him. But till that time abide ye at the court, there shall ye be well at ease in many ways. Now promise us this; we shall seek your father, and may we find him, and God give us honour in our quest, then will we return as swiftly as may be, and rejoice ye and the king!"

When the Moor heard these words he laughed with heart and mouth (his teeth were white as chalk, otherwise was he altogether black), and he spake, "God our Father reward ye, noble knights, for the good will and the honour ye have done me, and also for the great comfort wherewith ye have lightened mine heart that long hath been all too heavy. An my steed fail me not I shall ride whither ye bid me to this king whom ye praise so highly."

With that he pledged to the knights hand and knighthood, and called God to witness that he would do their bidding, faithfully, and without dispute, so long as he might live.

Then quoth Sir Lancelot: "Knight, an ye be in any need, when ye come into Arthur's land,—I ween 'tis all unknown to ye,—speak but of us twain whom ye see here and men shall do ye naught but honour and courtesy, where'er ye come, in any place. And when ye come to the king, ere ye tell him aught beside, say that ye have seen and have spoken with us; and trow me, without fail, ye shall be well received!" The Moor spake: "'Tis well said—God reward ye for this courtesy; but were it your will and pleasing to ye that I knew the names of ye two then i'sooth were I the blither withal!"

Then straightway Sir Gawain did him to wit who they were, and how they were hight; and the Moor made no delay, but fell on his knees before them. Sir Gawain raised him up, but the Moor laid his hands together and spake, "God the Father of all, and Ruler of the World, grant that I may amend my misdoing to your honour. Sir Lancelot, very dear lord, I own myself right guilty, for I did evil, and naught else!"

Sir Gawain spake: "Take ye not to heart that which has here chanced, it shall be naught the worse for ye."

Sir Gawain and Sir Lancelot were both mounted upon their steeds. The Moor spake: "'Tis labour lost. Such good knights as ye be, since ye at this time fare to seek my father, by the power of our Lord I will not stay behind; 'twere shame an I did. I shall ride with ye twain!"

Quoth Sir Gawain: "Then must ye lay aside all outrageousness, and ride peaceably on your way, and whatever knight shall meet ye, and greet ye courteously, him shall ye greet and let pass on his way without strife or contention; and be his friend an he hath done ye no wrong—this do I counsel ye straitly. But he that is fierce and fell towards ye or towards another, on him shall ye prove your prowess, and humble his pride, if ye may. And honour all women, and keep them from shame, first and last, as best ye may. Be courteous and of gentle bearing to all ye meet who be well-mannered toward ye, and he who hath no love for virtue against him spare neither sword, nor spear, nor shield!"

The Moor spake: "Since that ye will it so, I will at your bidding forbear, otherwise might I rue it! May God be gracious to me."

So rode they all three together till they came to a parting of the ways where stood a fair cross, and thereon letters red as blood. Sir Gawain was learned in clerkly lore, he read the letters wherein was writ that here was the border of Arthur's land, and let any man who came to the cross, and who bare the name of knight, bethink him well, since he might not ride far without strife and conflict, and the finding of such adventures as might lightly turn to his harm, or even to his death—the land was of such customs.

This did Sir Gawain tell to the twain. Then they saw, by the parting of the ways, a hermit's cell, fairly builded, and the knights bethought them that they would turn them thither that they might hear and see, and know what the words boded.

There saw they the hermit, who seemed to them a right good man; and they dismounted at his little window, and asked his tidings, if perchance a knight in red armour had passed that way? And the good man answered and said 'twas but the other day, afore noon, that he had seen two knights who were wondrous like unto each other. "Of a truth it seemed to me, by their features and by their gestures, that they should be brothers. Their steeds seemed beyond measure weary. They came that self-same road that cometh from that land that men here call Britain; they were both in seeming men of might, and the one had steed and armour that were even red as blood. They dismounted, both of them, at the foot of that cross ye see there. There many a judgment is given. There did a knight lose his life, he and his wife with him; well did they deserve that their memory should be held in honour by the friends of our Lord, for they made a right good ending! They had sought the shrine of a saint, with them they had money and steeds, beside other goods, as befitted folk of high degree. Here did they fall in with a company of robbers, who slew the good knight, and took his steed and his money, and all that he had. Of this was his wife so sorrowful that for grief and woe her heart brake, and so did they die here, the twain of them, even at the cross roads, where ye see the fair cross, where now many a judgment is spoken. 'Twas made through the knight's will. Hither come folk stripped and bare-foot, doing penance for their sins; and they who pass ahorse or afoot have here had many a prayer granted. The knights of whom ye ask did there their orisons, as well became them, but I may not tell ye whither they went at their departing; in sooth I know naught, for I said my prayers here within and forgat them. But they were tall and strong, and the one wore red armour, and the other bare the badge of King Arthur."

Then were the knights sorely grieved, and kindled as a coal for sorrow, in that they might not know, by any craft, whitherward they rode. Then they asked the manner of the land, and whither led the roads which they saw before them.

Then answered the good hermit, "I will tell ye as best I may. The road by which ye came, that do ye know; and the road that runneth straight therefrom that will ye shun, an ye heed my counsel. 'Tis a land of ill-fame, where men follow evil customs; their best, 'tis but others' worst! He who will keep his horse, his weapons and his life will shun that road. And the right-hand way goeth to a wild waste land, wherein no man dwelleth; an I bethink me well 'tis over a year and a day since I saw man or woman come from thence. An it so befall that ye fare thitherward ye shall find such a marvel that would ye dare the venture, and amend the wrong it shall cost ye life and limb, that do I tell ye here. For there shall ye find the most fell beast ever man heard or read of; take ye good heed thereof, 'tis the Foul Fiend himself, that know I well, that roameth in the guise of a beast. Against him may no weapon serve, there was never spear so sharp nor sword so well tempered, as I know of a truth, that may harm that devil, but it will break or bend as hath full oft been proven in time past. Now hath the beast chosen his dwelling in a little forest, there will he abide all night, but the day he prowleth by straight and winding ways. He devoureth man and beast alike, nor may I tell ye the marvels I have heard concerning him. He hath laid waste a broad land, and driven thereout all the country-folk, so that none remain. Now have I told ye the truth concerning these two roads, and what may befall ye therein; for the third, it leadeth hereby to the sea coast; I know not what I may say more."

Quoth Sir Lancelot: "By the Lord who made me, Sir Gawain, we must needs depart from each other here and now, would we find these knights. And I will dare that which I deem the most perilous venture. Ye shall ride straightway whichever road ye will, otherwise shall we lose the knights who were lately here, they shall not have ridden far as yet. And if it be that ye find them, then I charge and conjure ye, by my will and your valour, that if ye may, ye shall bring them with ye and return hither to this place. Do this, Sir Knight, for my prayer. And do the hermit to wit how matters have gone with ye, that he may tell me the truth thereof if peradventure I too come hither, and the knight shall go with ye, and God keep ye both since we be now come to this point. Do him honour as a good man and true, in whatsoever place ye may be, this I pray ye of your valour."

Sir Gawain gave him answer: "Dear comrade, I am fain to do your bidding, and may God keep us in life and limb, and in worldly honour. Now choose ye first which road ye will take, for here will we abide no longer."

Then said Sir Lancelot: "I ween that 'tis the most pressing need to go fight against the beast whereof the good man telleth us; methinks 'twere well that I ride thither."

And the hermit answered: "Alas, Sir Knight, ye be so fair that I deem below the throne one might scarce find your equal, and will ye brave a venture which no man may achieve! The folk hath fled out of the land, none may withstand that beast, no shaft is so fell as the venom which he shooteth on all who near him; and the man whom it reacheth, and upon whom it shall light (I am he who lieth not), he dieth ere the third day be past, had he never a wound upon him. This hath been the worse for many. Then is the beast greater than a horse, and runneth more swiftly than any horse may. Ye are wise an ye shun the fiend. This do I tell ye beforehand. Had he not chosen his lair, and did he wander from the land, as well might be, by the Lord who made us he had laid the world waste! Ye would do well to turn back."

But 'twas labour lost; not for all the riches that belonged to King Arthur would he have taken back his word and his covenant, for any prayer that might be made him, nor have yielded aught through fear.

Then would the knights take leave of each other that they might depart. The Moor spake to the twain: "For what do ye take me? Am I a lesser or a weaker man than either of ye that Sir Gawain must needs ride with me? I will not have it so. There is no knight so bold but I dare well withstand him. I know well what is unfitting. Now say whither ye will betake ye, and send me what road ye will; I will dare the venture, be it never so perilous. By my knighthood, and by all who follow Christendom, I shall adventure alone, and take that which may chance."

Then said Sir Gawain: "It liketh me ill that ye sware such an oath, yet since such is your will, take ye the road that leadeth to the sea (this seemeth to me the best), ride swiftly and spare not, but seek your father. And do in all things after my counsel; if any man meet ye, when ye have given him courteous greeting, ask him if he saw riding, or otherwise met with, two knights, the one of whom ware red armour, and the other bare King Arthur's badge. This shall ye first beseech of them. When ye come to the crossing, pray that men tell ye the truth, and ask for the sea-coast withal, wherever ye come. And if so be that men understand ye not then return straightway to this place, and follow the road which I shall take, swiftly, and with no delay. We might lightly depart so far from each other that we met not again. But follow me soon, and not too late; and do according as I counsel ye, and I tell ye truly, no harm shall befall ye."

The Moor spake: "God reward ye." Then took they leave each of the other, and departed asunder. Now will I tell ye how it fared with Sir Gawain.

The adventure telleth us forthwith that when prime was now already past Sir Gawain came to a wide and deep river. 'Twas a great stream, and deep, and the current ran swift and strong. Then Sir Gawain marked well, and took heed, how on the further side, in a land of which he knew naught, there came a knight riding on a fair steed, and armed as if for combat. Before him he drave captive a maiden. Sir Gawain beheld how he smote her, many a time and oft, blow upon blow, with his fist that weighed heavily for the mailed gauntlet that he ware. Pain enough did he make her bear for that she desired not to ride with him. He smote her many a time and oft with his shield as he would revenge himself upon her in unseemly fashion. The maiden ware a robe of green silk, that was rent in many places, 'twas the cruel knight had wrought the mischief. She rode a sorry hack, bare backed, and her matchless hair, which was yellow as silk, hung even to the horse's croup—but in sooth she had lost well nigh the half thereof, which that fell knight had afore torn out. 'Twas past belief, the maiden's sorrow and shame;

how she scarce might bear to be smitten by the cruel knight; she wept and wrung her hands.

This Sir Gawain beheld, and he deemed 'twere shame an he avenged not her wrong. He looked before and behind and saw no bridge, great or small, by which he might cross over, nor saw he living soul of whom he might ask, then did he delay no longer, but turned his bridle, and set his horse toward the river bank; he struck his spurs sharply and sprang into the midst of the stream. The good steed breasted the current, swimming as best it might and brought its master to the further side. 'Twas great marvel that they were not drowned, horse and man, for the river was deep, and the stream ran swiftly.

When Sir Gawain came to the other side of the river, which was both wide and deep, then saw he a great company of folk riding after the knight who bare away the maiden by force, and thus misused her, but he wist not if it was to aid the knight that they thus followed him, or to wreak vengeance on him. He saw many men clad in hauberks, but they were as yet a good mile distant. Sir Gawain rode swiftly after the maiden who went afore, whom the knight thus mishandled, to avenge her wrong; and as he drew near so that she might see him, she smote her hands together more than before, and cried to Gawain, "Noble knight, for the honour of womanhood, save me! This knight doeth me undeserved shame. Did there come hither any friend of God who would help me in this my need, an he had slain his own father it should be forgiven him!"

Her prayers and entreaties, her tears and lamentations, would have stirred any man to pity; she cried upon Sir Gawain as he came riding into the plain, to come to her aid and fell the knight's pride. As Sir Gawain heard her his heart was rent with sorrow and compassion and he spake to that evil knight: "Sir Knight, 'tis folly and discourtesy that which ye do to this maiden; were ye wise ye would forbear; even had the maiden wronged ye, ye should deal courteously; he hath small honour who thus smiteth a maiden."

Then said the cruel knight: "For ye, fool and meddler, whether ye be knight or no, will I not stay my hand, nay, rather for your shame, will I chastise her the more; and should ye but speak another word to her I shall thrust ye straightway from your steed with my spear!"

Quoth Sir Gawain: "Then were I but afoot Sir Knight! Natheless I counsel ye, an ye be wise, that ye spare the maiden. Ye will find me not so craven this day as to let ye harm her; I shall defend her and avenge her wrong if my life be risked upon it. But, Sir Knight, hearken to my prayer, for God and for your honour, and the sake of knighthood!"

But that evil knight answered and said he would in no wise do this: "An ye get not hence, and fly, by heaven it shall be your doomsday! I have no need of your sermons."

Quoth Sir Gawain: "An ye be so bold, lay but your hand again upon her, and I shall take so stern a pledge as, wist ye, shall dismay your heart, an it cost me my life. Let the maiden go in peace, or be on your guard against my spear, for I defy ye!"

The other was high and scornful that Sir Gawain so threatened him. He thought to quell his pride, and rode against him straightway, and Sir Gawain, on his side, did even the same. They came together so keenly that both spears brake, and the crash might be heard afar; they came together so swiftly that the knight was thrust from his saddle, and fell to the ground, and he fell so heavily that he felt the smart in every limb, and lay in anguish from the fall—so stayed he prone upon the ground.

Sir Gawain took the horse whereon the knight had ridden. He forgat not his courtesy, but gave it into the hand of the maiden, and drew forth his good sword. Therewith was the knight come to himself, and had taken his sword, and stood up as best he might. Evil was his thought, and he cried: "Vassal, how were ye so bold as to do me this hurt and this shame? My father is lord of this land, and after him shall it be mine. Think not to escape, 'tis folly that which ye do. Even to day shall ye be repaid by those who follow me, and chastised in such wise as ye would not have for all the riches King Arthur holds or ne'er may hold! My men will be here anon and ye shall not escape, for in this land hath no man power or might to withstand me."

Sir Gawain spake: "That may I well believe, and therefore are ye so cruel and so outrageous. That one who is noble of birth, and rich withal, should be false of heart, by my troth, 'tis great pity and bringeth many to shame. Now ye are not yet at such a pass but that I may teach ye moderation ere ye part from me. Methinks that to-day ye shall rue the evil ye have done. I counsel ye, an ye be wise, that ye make known to me wherein this lady hath wronged ye. Hath she indeed deserved that ye be thus cruel, then 'tis a matter 'twixt ye twain, I meddle no further. But hath the maiden not deserved this, then hold your hand, and make peace with me, otherwise is your life forfeit were ye never so highly born. I take the maiden with me when I ride hence." The knight would not hearken, and the maiden spake: "Noble knight I will tell ye wherefore he doeth me this wrong. He would have me for his love, why should I deny the truth? 'Tis many a day since he first spake to me, but I would not hearken to him, other sorrows vexed me; poverty grieveth me sore; thereto have I griefs that I may not lightly tell. My father was a knight, and a good man, and of high birth in this land. Dear Sir Knight, I will tell thee openly, though it be shame. My father hath lain sick, seven year long, and hath lost his goods, and now lieth in sore straits; he may neither ride nor walk nor stand upon his feet, he suffereth much. Now have I nursed and tended and otherwise served my father—friends hath he few save myself, and I had fain stayed by him and kept him all my life, doing for him all that within me lay. To-day came this knight within our hold, which is sore broken down and ruined, and hath done me sore wrong. He took me thence by force, ere I was well aware, nor stayed his hand for God or man. Thus did he carry me away, and now he doeth me this shame. He hath left his folk behind that they may hinder my friends, lest they follow him to his hurt. I fear lest they be here anon. And should they find ye here ye may scarce escape. Would ye save your life, then, Sir Knight, make a swift end of this combat. I fear it dureth over long an ye will aid me, by our Lord's grace. So bethink ye, Sir Knight, what ye may do."

Quoth Sir Gawain: "An ye be wise, Sir Knight, ye will now speak; here will I tarry no longer. Will ye right this maiden of the wrong ye have done her, or fight with me? The one or the other must ye do. An ye will, I will alight and meet ye afoot, or ye may mount your steed again, by covenant that ye flee not, nor escape, but abide your fortune."

The knight made answer: "Now do ye hold me over feeble, an ye think I shall thus yield. Ye will do well to dismount straightway, an ye have lust to fight." He covered himself with his shield, and drew forth his sword from the scabbard. Sir Gawain dismounted, whether he liked it well or ill, and let his horse that men call the Gringalet, stand beside him; never a foot would that steed stir till its lord came, and once more laid hand on it. Forthwith they betook them to fight, and dealt each other fierce thrusts, with mighty and strong strokes, so that one saw their blood stream out through the mails of their hauberk, and the sparks sprang out when the helmets were smitten till they seemed to glow even as doth hot iron when it be thrust into the furnace, and waxeth red from the fire; so fierce were the blows which each dealt to the other. That which most sorely vexed Sir Gawain was that his sword scarce seemed worth a groat, the knight's armour was so good that Sir Gawain's weapon was stayed upon it. Though one saw the blood well through, yet had the hauberk never a score. This Sir Gawain deemed a great marvel. He fetched a mighty blow upward and smote the knight above the hauberk, in the neck, to the very middle of the throat. Therewith was the matter ended for him; his head fell forward upon his breast, and he fell dead beneath the blow.

His friends and kinsmen had beheld from afar and came therewith, sore distressed and very wrath when they saw their lord thus lying dead upon the field. Sir Gawain, the good and the valiant, was once more mounted upon Gringalet. There might he fear no foe; the steed was so strong and so great, and even as his lord had need would the horse watch and follow every sign that he might give.

Those who had come thither, and had, as it were, found Sir Gawain in the very act of slaying, were of one mind that they should beset him, behind and afore, on horse and afoot, and if it might be take his life. And Sir Gawain who saw that he was sore bestead, commended himself to the grace of God with a good heart and received his foes with drawn sword. With each blow that he smote he wounded one, or two, and wrought them much harm. None might withstand him, and he that wrought the most valiantly he abode there dead, or went hence so sorely wounded that he might never more find healing. Thus Gawain, the Father of Adventure, so daunted them with the blows that he smote that many drew aside and turned from the strife with deep wounds and wide. 'Twas a good cause for which Sir Gawain fought, and for which he desired vengeance, and for that did it fall to his profit. He brought many of them in sore stress, some of life, some of limb. With that there came riding a company of the maiden's folk, who were fain to avenge her shame. So soon as she beheld them, and they drew nigh, was she glad and blithe and drew aside from the strife where Sir Gawain did right manfully. The maiden turned to her own folk, and betook her with that company again to her father. They were right joyful that she was once more in their power, and they left Sir Gawain on the field where he was sore bestead—they durst not take part with him against their overlord, so greatly did they fear his kin.

But Sir Gawain, who marked this not, went smiting blow after blow on all that came nigh him, and so blinded and drave them backward with his strokes that he was left alone on the field. So weary and so weak were they that they lay all along the road, discomfited, prone on the earth, as those who have sore need of rest. But few of them were whole, for Sir Gawain had so wounded them that men may well tell the tale from now even unto Doomsday!

Then thought Sir Gawain within himself, since he had so long wielded his weapons and no man durst withstand him further he might find no better counsel than to fare on his way. He thanked God of true heart that he had thus won honour on this evil folk, and that he had escaped with his life, and free from mortal wound, he and his steed, and that God had thus protected them. Men say oft, and 'tis true, as was here well proven, that he who recks not of his ways, but doeth that which is displeasing alike to God and to the world, he was born in an evil hour.

Now when Sir Gawain had won the fight, and God had shown him favour by granting him good knighthood and the discomfiting of his foes, the day was well past nones, and Sir Gawain, the bold, had neither eaten nor drunk, nor done aught save fight that day and receive great blows. He rode on his way sore perplexed and unknowing where he might seek for lodging. So long did he ride that he was ware how it drew towards evening, and therewith did he behold a castle. Never was a man more oppressed with hunger and thirst and weariness; and he thought in his heart that he could do naught better than ride thither, and see if by hap he might find lodging for the night.

He found by the castle moat the lord of that burg and many of his folk with him; when he had dismounted on the turf he greeted them courteously, and the lord answered "God reward ye."

Quoth Sir Gawain, "Were it your command, and your will and pleasure, right gladly would I abide here within this night! I know not otherwise how I may win shelter. I have ridden all this day, and have seen naught save wilderness and waste land, and there found I no man with whom I might abide the night."

And the host spake, "So may good befall me in soul and body as I shall give to you in friendship, even to the uttermost, all that belongeth unto this even; lodging will I give ye, and food, ham and venison. My lodging is ever free, and ne'er refused to any knight who would fain be my guest. He hath safe conduct, good and sure, against all whom he may meet in this land, were it against mine own son, whom I love above all who own the laws of knighthood. My safe conduct is so well assured that whosoe'er should wrong my guest it should cost him his life and all that he had, had he not more than good fortune! This on my knighthood and by the Blessed Maid, Our Lady!"

But Sir Gawain, the Father of Adventure, who was wont to be received with honour, wist not that the knight whom he had slain was son to the lord of the castle. Now first shall ye hear of marvellous adventures whereof some be good and some evil.

Sir Gawain had come to that point that he deemed he was well assured of shelter for the night, nor was he on guard against his heavy mischance. The host, who would do his guest all honour, took the knight by the hand, and led him through three portals into a fair hall where he was received with courteous words. They disarmed him straightway, and stabled his steed right well. The host bade them take in ward Sir Gawain's armour and his sword; too far did they carry them! For that was he vexed and wrathful, and he would not it had so chanced for all his host's halls, were they of wroughten gold! For as they sat at table and ate and drank and had enow of all the earth might bear for the sustenance of man, and forgat thereby all sorrow, they heard sore wailing and lamentation, and the smiting together of hands, and knew not what it might mean. They heard folk who stood without the walls, at the master gate, who cried with loud voice, "Alas, alas! Undo and let us in!"

Then Sir Gawain's mood was changed, and his heart forbade him that sorrow and mischief drew near. He changed colour and grew red. The lord gave command from within that they should ask what company stood without, and what tidings they bare. Then they sprang to the gate, and opened it, even as their lord bade.

Then came they in, who stood without, bearing a bier, and making so great cry and lamentation that men heard it far and near through the open doorways. So came they into the hall, a great company of folk, and cried with a loud voice to the lord of the castle, "Alas, master, here lieth dead the best knight that one might find in the wide world, even your dear son. There liveth not his like on earth, so strong, so bold, so skilled in valiant deeds!"

Then was all the burg aghast; and the host, the father of the knight who lay dead upon the bier, felt his heart die within him. Scarce might he find words; and he cried, "Who hath robbed him of life, mine own dear son, whom I loved above all the world? How came he by his death? I fear me 'twas by his own deed, for well I know that he was fierce of heart, and spared neither foe nor friend. I fear lest he have merited his death. Now do I conjure ye all here present, by God, our Righteous Father (so spake the lord of the castle) that ye speak, and make known to me the whole truth; fain would I hear how he came by his death, my dear son, who lieth here, and for whom my heart doth sorely grieve."

Then said they all who brought the dead man thither, that forsooth 'twas a stranger knight who did this by his great valour; "Though we saw it not with our eyes, yet may we well bear witness to the death of many of our folk; and others are so sorely wounded that they may never more be healed. Man may scarce tell all the mischief wrought by that stranger knight who slew your son, the best knight on earth; nor may we tell who he might be." But Sir Gawain, who was there within, and knew well that he was guilty, saw that he might scarce escape either by will or by valour, since he had laid aside his weapons and stood all unarmed in his robes; thereof was he grieved at heart.

As they stood and spake thus, sudden they saw the blood of the knight who lay there dead, and which afore was stanched, leap forth afresh, and run crimson down the hall. With this were they ware of Sir Gawain, their lord's guest, and all they who were there present said, the one taking up the tale of the other, that forsooth he who had slain the knight was within that hall, as might be seen of men, for the blood had ceased to flow a little after midday, nor had any man seen the wounds bleed since. Now was it open and manifest to all that he was there who had done the deed. Herein were they all of one mind who were there present, and they drew together and looked upon Sir Gawain the Father of Adventure, with fierce and cruel eyes.

Sir Gawain saw many an unfriendly countenance turned towards him. They straitly prayed their lord that he would make the knight known to them; how he came thither; who he was, whence he came, and whither he went, and what might be his name?

Then spake the host: "He is my guest, and he hath my safe conduct, good and fast, the while he is within; and be ye sure of this, that if any wrong him by word or deed, he shall rue it in such wise that it shall cost him goods and life. Nor will I change for prayer of man or woman. My surety that I will hold to every guest standeth so fast that no word I have spoken shall be broken with my knowledge or my will. Have patience and hold ye still, on peril of your lives and goods. I know so good counsel withal that I may speedily be ware of him who hath wrought this deed."

Then he called together his folk to one side of the hall, and said that his oath and his safe conduct might in no wise be broken, for his son were thereby but ill-avenged, valiant knight though he was. He might well rue it if he slew his guest, for thereof should he have great shame wherever men told the tale. "I shall avenge him more discreetly, if I be well-assured of the truth that my guest hath indeed wrought this murder and this great outrage."

He spake further to his folk: "Now do ye all my bidding. Ye shall abide here within this hall; no man shall follow me a foot, but do ye even as I command. I will lead my guest without, and ye shall close the door behind us. Doth the dead man cease to bleed, then shall we all be well-assured that he hath done the deed; and thereafter shall I take counsel how I may avenge my son, fittingly, and without shame." Then all agreed to his counsel, and held their peace.

Thus came the host to where Sir Gawain stood, and spake: "Sir Knight, be not wroth that my folk entreat ye not better. We are in grief, as ye see, and therefore are ye the worse served. Now shall ye come with me, and I shall amend what hath here been lacking. My folk and my household make great lamentation, as ye see, and I with them. Now come with me, and tarry not; I will lead ye hence where ye may be at ease, and sleep softly till the daylight. Here would we make our moan."

Sir Gawain thought within himself he was sorely over-matched within those (to be bare of weapons 'tis a heavy blow at need), and he knew well that the folk looked on him with unfriendly eyes, and that none were on his side, that might be seen from their mien; and therefore he thought within himself that there was no better counsel save to put himself in his host's grace, and do that which he bade him. He had no weapon upon him, and there were within of his host's folk full five hundred men whom he saw to be armed. Thus he went his way with his host, whether the adventure should turn to his harm or to his helping. The lord of the castle led him through the doorway, and his men locked it as they went forth.

Then quoth the lord of those within: "Sir Knight and dear guest, I will that ye be right well entreated here within this night." He led him to a strong tower, wherein were fair beds. He bade them bear tapers before them, and all that he knew or could in any wise deem needful for Sir Gawain, his guest. The host, sorely mourning, bade them pour out clear wine, and make ready a fair couch whereon he might sleep even as he had the will thereto. He left with him squires enow, and turned him again to the castle.

Then did they bear the dead man from where he lay, his wounds were stanched, and bled no whit. Then said all who saw it it booted not to seek another man, they were well assured 'twas their guest had slain him. The word ran through the hall; and the host turned him again to where he had left his guest, as if he marked naught. He made no sign to his folk, but locked the door of the tower so fast that none might come therein to Sir Gawain to do him harm, nor overpower him, so safely was he in his keeping. Also, I tell ye, he himself kept the keys of the strong tower wherein he had locked his guest. He would bethink him what 'twere best to do ere he let him be slain or maimed; thus did he hold him within his fortress.

What might Sir Gawain do? He must even abide his fate; he had come thither as guest, and now was he locked in a strong tower, within many doors, and in a strange place withal. He was bare of arms, and had he revealed himself and demanded his weapons they had scarce given them to him; rather had they slain him, and drawn blood-guiltiness upon themselves had not God protected him.

Thus was Sir Gawain a captive, and knew not what he might do. 'Twixt constraint and ill-fortune the night seemed to him over long; though he feared him no whit yet he deemed his end was come. He knew well that the folk were evil-disposed and bare malice and rancour towards him for the sake of the dead man who lay there, in that they had seen his wounds bleed afresh, and had thereby known his slayer. Thus was his heart sorely troubled.

Now leave we speaking of Sir Gawain. The host was within the hall, with his folk until daylight; with sorrow and lamentation did they pass the night, bemoaning their bitter loss. For though the knight had well deserved his death yet had he there many friends who lamented the loss that they had thereby suffered. They were loth to own that he was evil and cruel of heart.

So soon as they saw the fair day light the host took counsel with his folk that they might advise him well by what means, and in what way, they might avenge themselves for their heavy loss. Said the host, their lord, did he let the guest, whom he held there captive, and who had smitten his son to death, depart in safety, "Men would say I were but a coward, and durst not avenge myself, and would speak scorn of me; so many have seen how the matter fell out that it may not well remain hidden. Yet should I slay my guest then from henceforward would they cry shame upon me in every land where the tale be told."

Thus was he of two minds, and thought in his heart that to save himself from shame 'twere best to let his guest depart so soon as he arose, armed in all points as he came thither, and harm him in no wise, but bring him, unhurt by any man, without the borders of his land and his safe conduct, and there bid him farewell and return hither; while that his friends, who would fain see him avenged, waylaid Sir Gawain, and wrought their will upon him, and, if they would, slew him. Or if they took him captive they might deal with him as they thought best, either by burning him in the fire, to cool their rage, or by breaking him upon the wheel —as might seem best to them at the time. "Thus shall I put the shame from me, that neither near nor afar, now or henceforward, men make scorn of me. This seemeth to me the wisest rede in this matter, howsoe'er it stand!"

This did he tell to his folk, and it pleased them well, and they spake with one mouth that he had found the best counsel. They made no further questioning, but armed themselves, and rode forth, as they who would waylay Sir Gawain, when his host had sent him on his way. Thus they went forth from thence a great company, and well armed. Very wrathful were they, and they went right willingly. The host who would follow them called to him his seneschal, who was cruel and cunning, and bade him carry his armour to their guest straightway, and deliver it to him as if he should ride thence as soon as he had arisen, and delay no whit.

Straightway the seneschal betook him to a fair chamber (hearken ye to an evil tale!) where he found Sir Gawain's weapons and his good armour. He stole from Sir Gawain his good sword, that which he placed in its sheath was not worth twopence; he cut the straps of the harness well nigh in twain in the midst, and made a great score in the stirrup leathers so cunningly that no man might see or know aught thereof beneath the covering of the harness. And the saddle-girths did the traitor so handle that Sir Gawain was sore grieved there-for ere he had ridden a mile; he would not that it had so chanced for all King Arthur's kingdom—that shall ye hear anon.

When the seneschal who had wrought this treason had brought Sir Gawain's weapons and his horse that had been well cared for that night—they deemed it should be theirs ere long, 'twas a strong steed and well standing, and since they thought to have their pleasure of it they gave it provender enow—the host bade them undo the door and hold Sir Gawain's steed there without.

The harness was in place, whereof I have told ye that it was so traitorously handled; then came forth the knight, who had arisen, and clad himself in fair robes, and descended the stairway. Little thought had he of the treason which in short while befell him. The seneschal held in his hand the false sword, well hidden in its sheath, and the while Sir Gawain made him ready did he gird it at his side—for that was the knight thereafter unblithe.

The while they thus made ready came the lord of the castle to Sir Gawain, and said: "Ye are early astir Sir Knight; how comes it that ye be thus hurried at this time? Scarce have ye slept, and arisen, ere ye would ride hence. Have ye heard Mass, and broken your fast ere ye depart?"

Quoth Sir Gawain: "Dear mine host, I grieve that ye yet sorrow; so may God guard me and bring me to His grace when I die as I truly mourn for your mischance. I will it were yet to do!" Quoth Sir Gawain the bold: "Though 'twere hard and painful to me yet would I for seven years long wear haircloth next my body, wherever I fared, for this that ye have received me so well. Nevertheless be ye sure of a truth—I may not deny it this day for any man, how strong soever he might be, nor through fear of any that may hear me, foe or friend—but I must needs say in sooth your son had merited his death many a time and oft ere the day came that he died! Now may God have mercy upon him! And God reward ye for the great good, and the honour, that ye do to me, all ye here, in that I have been at your charges."

Then was the host sore vexed, and he said: "I will do ye no harm for aught that hath chanced by ye; nevertheless, there be here many a man who had fain fallen upon ye, but I tell ye I will not that aught befall ye here; nor that my peace be broken, nor vengeance taken upon ye. I shall go with ye as ye ride hence, and ride with ye so far that ye be not led astray by any who remain behind. I were loth that harm befell ye."

Sir Gawain spake: "For that may God, who ruleth over all, reward ye." He took the bridle in his hand and rode forth, the host nigh to him; and at his side went he who had betrayed him aforehand. Now cometh great sorrow upon Sir Gawain. He deemed that he had safe conduct, but he had lost from its sheath his sword, which had been stolen from him; and that which the seneschal had put in its place when he drew forth the good brand was more brittle than glass. Thereto had he cunningly handled the harness, girths and stirrup-leather, whereof Sir Gawain knew naught, and the lord of the castle had sent afore the strongest and most valiant of his folk, to waylay Sir Gawain, and to take his life, A man's heart might well fail him for doubt, and great fear, did he come in such a pass, and know no wile whereby he might escape.

Sir Gawain, who knew naught of these tricks and snares rode on his way, discoursing of many things with his host, until they drew nigh to the place where his foes lay, ambushed in the thicket, who would fain slay him. When he came nigh to the place the host took leave of the knight, and turned him again towards the castle. Sir Gawain sat upon his steed and deemed that he should ride thence without strife or combat. As he laid his hand on the saddle-bow, and thrust his feet into the stirrups and thought to rise in the saddle, the girths brake asunder, the saddle turned over the left stirrup beneath the horse, and left him standing. Then Sir Gawain saw a great company of folk spring forth and come towards him with all their might. Some came from the ditches where they had lain hidden, some out of bushes, some out of thickets, and some came forth from the hollow ways. God confound traitors, since He may not mend them!

Sir Gawain abode not still; he saw well that he was betrayed, and over-matched. He drew forth from its sheath the sword, which was little worth to him, and deemed he would defend himself, as he oft had done aforetime, against those who would harm him. But ere he might smite three blows that sword brake, as it were tin—this was an ill beginning would a man defend his life. This Sir Gawain saw, and was dismayed, he wist well that he was betrayed. They who would harm him came upon him from every side, a great company and fierce, all thirsting for his life; there was a great clash of swords; they thrust at him with their spears. His sword protected him not a whit—he who gave it to him God give him woe! It brake in twain at the hilt, and fell into the sand. Sir Gawain stood empty-handed, small chance had he of escape, and they who beset him were chosen men, over-strong and over-fierce, as was there well proven. Like as a wild boar defends himself against the hounds that pursue him, even so did Sir Gawain defend himself, but it helped him naught. They harmed him most who stood afar, and thrust at him with spears to sate their rage. There was among them no sword so good but had Sir Gawain held it, and smote with it three such blows as he was oft wont to deal with his own, it had broken, or bent, and profited them no whit. But of those things which had stood him in good stead many a time before, when he was hard beset, his good steed, and his sword, the which was a very haven, of these was he now robbed.

Thus was Sir Gawain overcome, and me thinks 'twas little marvel! There lives no man so strong or so valiant but he may some time be vanquished by force, or by fraud. Sir Gawain must needs yield him; he was felled to the ground, yet were there some to whom it cost their life ere he was captive, and some it cost a limb, or twain, that might never more be healed; and he himself was so sore mishandled that all he ware, whether it were armour or other clothing, was rent in many a place, so that the flesh might be seen. There lived on earth no man so wise that he might aid him in this stress, nor leech who might heal him; yet, an God will, he shall be healed of his smart and of his shame.

They bound Sir Gawain's hands, and set him on a sorry hack, and to anger him they led beside him Gringalet, his steed. This they did that he might be the more sorrowful when he beheld his horse, which he had now lost, and his own life withal! For of this would they deprive him, and make him to die a shameful death; burn him they would, or break him upon the wheel, that they might wreak their vengeance upon him. There were among them knights and squires, the richest, and the most nobly born after the lord of the land; and all had sworn an oath that they would lead Sir Gawain to the cross-roads, at the entering in of their land for the greater shaming of King Arthur's Court. To this had they pledged themselves, that they would there slay him without respite or delay; and were it not that 'twere shame to themselves, and too great dishonour to one who bare the name of knight, they had hung him by the neck, on the border of the two lands, to shame King Arthur; so that all his folk who were of the knightly order, and dwelt at his court, and sought for adventure, should shun their land when they heard the tidings of the vengeance wrought by them upon knights-errant who would prove their fate within those borders.

Thus it fell out that they brought Sir Gawain on the horse, sorely wounded and mishandled, within the nearness of half a mile, so that the knight knew he was nigh to the cell of the Hermit of whom at that self-same cross-road he had asked tidings of King Arthur's knights, and of that bad and evil land where many were brought to shame. And they who had brought him thither were of one mind that they should make a wheel, and break the knight upon it at the Cross by the parting of the ways whereof I have told ye afore.

Now shall I leave speaking of this matter till I come again thereto, and will forthwith tell ye how it fared with Morien when the three had parted asunder, as I told ye afore (Sir Gawain, Morien, and Sir Lancelot, he was the third), since they would fain make proof of that which the Hermit had told them. Now will I tell ye of Morien ere that I end the tale of Sir Gawain.

Now doth the adventure tell that Morien, that bold knight, rode the seaward way, and came safely to the passage of the ford nigh unto the open sea. And all the day he met no man of whom he might ask concerning his father; 'twas labour wasted, for all who saw him fled from him. Little good might his asking do him, since none who might walk or ride would abide his coming. But he saw there the hoof-prints of horses, which lay before him and were but newly made; by this he deemed that his father had passed that way but a short while before.

Thus he followed the hoof-tracks to the passage of the sea. That night had he neither rest nor slumber, nor found he place where he might shelter, or where it seemed to him he might ask for food or lodging beneath a roof.

The morning early, even as it dawned and men might see clearly and well (which comforted him much), he came safely ahorse to where one might make the crossing, but he saw never a soul; no man dwelt thereabout, for the robbers had laid waste the land, and driven away the folk so that none remained. 'Twas all heath and sand, and no land beside; there grew neither barley nor wheat. He saw and heard no man, nor did folk come and go there, but he saw ships at anchor, and shipmen therein, who were wont to take over those folk who would cross into Ireland.

Morien came riding over the sea-sand, and cried with a loud voice shipward: "Ye who be within tell me that which I ask lest it be to your own loss, as also I would fain know for my own profit and rejoicing. Know ye if any within these few days past have carried a knight over the water?"

But all they who lay in the ships, when they beheld Morien who had doffed his helm, were so afeard for him that they might neither hear nor understand question nor answer. They were altogether in fear of him, since he was so tall, and black withal. Each man turned his boat seaward, and put off from the shore, for Morien was to look upon even as if he were come out of hell. They deemed they had seen the Foul Fiend himself, who would fain deçeive them, so they departed as swiftly as they might and would in no wise abide his coming. Then must Morien turn him again, for none would hearken to his speech nor tell him that which he fain would know; all were of one mind that 'twas the Devil, and none else, who rode there upon the sand, so they fled with one consent from the shore.

Morien saw well that his labour was in vain, for would he make the crossing there was no man would abide his coming or receive him into his boat. Thus must he needs turn him back, and great lamentation did he make thereof. He saw the footprints where two horses had ridden afore him, and ever he hoped that 'twas his father who rode there, and that he had crossed the water, but he thought within himself: "What doth it profit a man to labour if he know it to be in vain? None will take me over the water since I am a Moor, and of other countenance than the dwellers in this land; this my journey is for naught. I may not do better than return to the Hermit, that good man, there where I parted from my comrades." He had neither eaten nor drunk since that he rode thence; his head was dazed with hunger and with grief. He looked behind and afore, and saw nowhere where food was in preparing, nor saw he man nor woman, nor creature that had life, upon the seashore.

Then he rode swiftly upon the backward trail till he came once more to the parting of the ways; there found he carpenter-folk hewing and shaping timber, whereof they had made a great wheel. He saw a knight sitting upon the ground, in sore distress, naked and covered with blood; he had been brought thither to be broken upon the wheel, so soon as it might be made ready. Well might his heart misgive him!

Morien who came thither saw the gleam of many a hauberk; there were armed folk enow! Others there were who were but in evil case, unarmed, and unclad, who were scarce whole. Their limbs were bandaged, some the arm, some the leg, some the head, and stained with blood. And Sir Gawain, who sat there sore mishandled, knew that well, and as Morien came nigh, he cried, so that all might hear: "Dear my comrade, ye be welcome. God give me joy of your coming hither! I am Gawain, your comrade; little did I foresee this mischance when we parted, you and I, at this cross-way! Have pity upon the sore stress in which ye see me. May God who hath power over us all strengthen ye well; would that He might here show forth His power!"

When Morien who was hard beset by them who stood there heard this, never might one hear in book or song that any man smote such fierce blows as he smote with the sword which he drew forth. Do what he might with that sword it suffered neither dint nor scar; he smote straight to the mid-ward; nor was their harness so good that it might withstand him. Thereto helped his great strength, that he fought so fiercely against them who withstood him, and smote such ghastly wounds that nevermore might they be healed, nor salved by the hand of any leech. He clave many to the teeth, through helm and coif, so that they fell to the ground. And ever as he cast his eyes around and they lighted upon Sir Gawain, who was in such evil case, his courage waxed so great that were the Devil himself against him he had slain him even as a man; might he die, he had there lost his life. Sir Gawain sat by the wayside in sorry plight, with his hands bound; but the good knight Morien so drave aback the folk who had brought him thither that they had little thought for him. He defended him so well with his mighty blows that none might come at him to harm him; he felled them by twos and by threes, some under their horses, some beside them. The space began to widen round Sir Gawain and Morien; for all there deemed that he came forth from hell, and was hight Devil, in that he so quelled them and felled them underfoot that many hereafter spake thereof. That men thrust and smote at him troubled him little, therein was he like to his father, the noble knight Sir Agloval; he held parley with no man, but smote ever, blow after blow, on all who came nigh him. His blows were so mighty; did a spear fly towards him, to harm him, it troubled him no whit, but he smote it in twain as it were a reed; naught might endure before him. He ware a hauberk that bold overstrong hero, wherewith he was none too heavy laden, yet none might harm him with any weapon they brought thither. Then might ye see the blood run red upon the ground for the good knight's sword spared neither horse nor man. There might ye see lying heads and hands, arms and legs; some hewn from the body, some smitten in twain. They who might escape death fared little better, for good fortune had departed from them —thus many chose their end. He who came betimes to the conflict, and fled without waiting to see what might chance further, he was blithe! Thus were they put to rout, and either slain or driven from the field, or helpless of limb; some who came thither ahorse had lost their steeds, and must rue their journey. They might no longer ride, but must go hence afoot.

Then Morien dismounted, and took Sir Gawain in his arms, and said full oft, "Alas, my comrade, how were ye thus betrayed? I fear physician may aid ye never more, ye have wounds so many and so sore."

With that he had unbound his hands; and Sir Gawain said: "Of physician have I no need." He thanked God and Morien a hundredfold, that he was thus delivered from peril, and comforted in his need; his heart was light within him, and he said he should speedily mend might he but have repose for two days, and neither walk nor ride; by the help of God, and by leechcraft and the aid of certain herbs the virtue of which he knew well, so might he regain all his strength.

Now had they left upon the field Gringalet and certain other steeds, the masters whereof were slain or had fled afar. Gringalet was bare of harness, he had lost his saddle as ye heard afore, and therefore no man had mounted him. He who had brought him thither had forgat him upon that field, his journey had been dearly bought and he lay there dead in the green grass. And Sir Gawain when he was ware of that was fain to forget all his pain. He arose from where he sat, and went towards his steed, and as he looked upon him his heart rose high within him, and he deemed that he was well-nigh healed. And even as he came Gringalet knew his lord, nor would flee from him, but came towards him, and for very friendship seized him with his teeth.

Then did they abide no longer, but betook them to the hermit who had been sore afeard for all that he heard and saw through the window of his cell. He knew the two knights well, when he heard their tale, and how that they were even the same who had but lately passed his way, and he spake to the Father of Adventure: "Even so did I foretell ye when ye would ride toward that land, and I prayed ye to refrain. But that would ye not do, and so have ye come to harm therein! They who are fain to despise counsel ofttimes do so to their own mischief. But since it hath so befallen, think ye what may best profit ye, and abide overnight with me, here within; for an ye depart hence I know not where ye may find shelter. That evil beast whereof I spake when ye were here afore hath so laid waste the land that no man dwelleth herein. If I still dwell here 'tis that I have no need to flee nor to fear death ere my day come, when as it hath been foretold and declared I shall break the rule of my order. A long tale is ill to hear, I will weary ye not, but see that naught be lacking to your ease. Ye shall stable your steeds, and abide this night within my chapel. That which I have will I give ye, for the love of God and the honour of knighthood." Then Sir Gawain and Morien his comrade thanked him much, and went their way to the chapel, where they abode throughout the day; each told to the other his adventures as they had befallen, neither more nor less. The hermit tended the horses well with all that was needful to them; he bade the lad who served him, as a good man doth his friend, bring forth all the store that he had within, and fetch water from the spring, and warm it to Sir Gawain's liking that he might therewith wash his limbs, and cleanse them from the blood. He had upon him no mortal wound, so good was his hauberk, otherwise had he lost his life from the blows he had received.

With that came the hermit into the chapel, and spake, and told them how he had heard tidings from pilgrims who had come thither that the Red Knight and his companions had but late ridden the road that led toward the sea coast, though he had marked it not; 'twas but yesterday he had been told thereof.

Then spake the knight Morien and said by his troth he had even followed the hoof prints of horses that were but newly made till he came to where one must needs cross over the water; "and then did I lose all sign of their further track; but howsoever I might pray, or call upon those who lay there in their ships, when they saw me they were terrified as hares, and would tell me nought, the fools, of that I asked them! One and all fled, and put them out to sea. Methinks they were afraid of me. But by the faith that I owe to God and Our Lady, and the honour of knighthood, it shall avail them naught that they thus refuse me; I shall turn again from here, and otherwise take my way; may I but find on shore one of those who were there, and who belongeth to the ships, in sooth he were born in an evil hour! An he carry me not over the water I will thrust him through with my spear, or deal him such a stroke with my sword, that he shall fall dead upon the earth. My heart forbode me that he who went before me was my father! But in all my journey I met no living soul of whom I might ask aught. Then I began to wax fearful, for hunger beset me, and therein I found neither man nor woman, nor aught but heather and waste land wherein I was a stranger. No man might I see or hear, no wheat or barley grew there; 'tis the truth I tell ye, thither cometh no man save that he desire to cross the wide water in the ships that there lie ready. Thus had I my pain for naught. But whatsoe'er befall me since that I have heard from our host, that good man, that my father in sooth rode that way I shall follow hard after, if so be that I may but cross over, and will but await tomorrow's dawn. Since that I have heard he rideth not so far ahead I may well overtake him, an my steed, which is so swift, and strong, and good, foil me not!"

"God speed ye!" quoth Sir Gawain. Such was indeed his counsel, and he sore lamented his own evil plight. But ill had it chanced with him; within the castle had they stolen from him his good sword wherewith he should defend himself. God give him shame who stole it! His saddle-girth, his stirrup-leathers, were cut midway through; as he thought to sit upon his steed they brake clean in twain, and left him standing upon his feet. This did Sir

Gawain tell them there, even as ye have heard aforetime. If his heart were heavy when he took count of this, 'twas small marvel!

Then did they wash Sir Gawain's limbs, and he himself searched his wounds. So good a leech might no man find since the day of Mother Eve as was Sir Gawain; whatever wound he tended, 'twas healed even as ye looked upon it!

That night had they all the comfort that the hermit might prepare till that they saw the fair day dawn and the sun begin to rise. Sir Gawain was somewhat troubled, since he lacked alike arms and clothing: also his wounds, which were sore, pained him the more. Nor did there live any near at hand whom he knew, and who might give them what was lacking. Neither bread, meat, nor wine had they; naught remained to the hermit, he had given the knights all his store. Morien's heart was set upon following his father, and Sir Gawain was of a mind to ride in quest of Sir Lancelot, and learn how it had fared with him. He was loth to delay or abide there, for he would fain, so soon as he might ride, fare in search of his comrade. Yet must he tarry a day ere he might mount his steed, such was his stress from the wounds he had received—sooth, it was a marvel that he escaped! And now food had failed them, and that was a sore lack. Even had they money or pledge to offer there dwelt none that side of the border, as they too well knew, but their bitter foes, who had fain wrought them woe. 'Twas seven miles and more hard riding, ere they might find village or fort in King Arthur's land. Hereof was Sir Gawain troubled. He might neither ride nor walk for his own aid. Thus both were ill at ease and sore oppressed.

Morien was loth to remain, yet he thought it shame to forsake his comrade, Sir Gawain, and thus he abode with him in the chapel.

Then as Morien stood by the window, it seemed to him that he saw a knight come riding in great haste, on a horse tall and swift; he was well armed, and seemed a goodly knight withal. Morien spake to Sir Gawain as he lay there. "What may this be? Here cometh a knight, and I know not whither he goeth!"

Sir Gawain abode not still, but went as best he might to the window; he looked upon the knight, and deemed by his armour and the tokens whereby a man may be known of men, that 'twas his own brother, Sir Gariët, the son alike of his father and of his mother. He came riding, as one sore pressed, on that self-same road that led from Britain. The more Sir Gawain looked upon him the more he deemed he knew him; and when he came nigh to the Hermitage he knew well the arms that he bare. Then was Sir Gawain gladder at heart than I may tell ye, for Sir Gariët his brother, that strong and valiant knight, brought with him that of which they were sorely in need, bread and meat, and wine fresh and clear.

'Twas sore need brought him hither, as ye shall now hear: They of Britain had lost King Arthur their lord, and were in sore danger of losing all their land, therefore had they sent Sir Gariët to seek Sir Gawain, and Sir Lancelot, since they twain were without peer, the most valiant knights of the court. Sir Perceval might well be accounted the third, but 'twas not for long that he practised knighthood; nevertheless he brought many into sore stress, even as ye have heard.

When Sir Gariët had come before the hermitage, Sir Gawain came forth with haste from the chapel on to the road, as one who was blithe beyond measure when he beheld his brother; and he said, "God give ye good day, that ye come, brother, and that I see ye! Never was I so joyful of aught, since that I was born."

Sir Gariët alighted on the turf when he saw his brother; and as he came nigh to him he took him in his arms saying: "Alas, brother, woe is me! How hath this so chanced? Methinks ye have suffered harm, and been in such sore strife that 'tis a marvel an ye be healed, and escape with life, ye seem to me in such evil case." Thus spake Sir Gariët. And Sir Gawain said, "I have never a limb but feeleth the smart of wounds, yet am I whole of heart, and shall heal myself right well. But let that tale be, and make known to me the errand upon which ye ride that ye be now come hither. Fain would I know the truth."

Quoth Sir Gariët, "That will I tell ye."

Thus went the twain into the chapel, where they found that good man, the hermit, and Morien, who was black of face and of limb. Then was Sir Gariët somewhat in fear, when he saw him so great of limb and of such countenance. This marked well his brother, Sir Gawain, and he gave him to wit of the knight, and of his name, who he was, and whence he came, ere he asked him aught;

for he saw well that he somewhat misdoubted him when he saw the good knight Morien of such countenance.

So sat they down together, and each bade the other welcome, and made much joy of their meeting. But Sir Gawain was more desirous than I may tell ye of knowing wherefore Sir Gariët, his brother, came thither, till he brought him to that point that he spake the truth concerning what had chanced to King Arthur, and told how the worst had befallen him. "King Arthur is taken captive! As he fared on a day to hunt in a great forest, as he was wont to do, there came upon him the greatest company of armed men that I may tell ye of, in these few words, who were all the King of the Saxons' men. They were in such force that they took King Arthur, who foresaw naught of this, and had but few folk with him, as he but went a-hunting. Thereof are his people sore troubled, and the queen above all—she is well nigh distraught in that the king is captive. She knows not whither the folk who took him in the forest have led him, or what may since have befallen him. Thereof is many a heart sorrowful. The forest standeth by the sea shore, whence came the folk who took the king by force, and led him whither they would. They who rode with King Arthur were unarmed, and defenceless; their strength was not worth a groat. Thereto have we another woe; the Irish King hath come into the land, and made war; one town hath he already won, and layeth siege to another. He hath made his boast that he will win all Arthur's land, hill and vale, castle and town (this is his intent), and bring all under his hand ere he quit our land. Of this is the queen sore afraid, and they who be with her, they look not to escape. Had ye, brother, been in the land, and Perceval, and Lancelot, then had we never come to such a pass, for there liveth no man so bold that he durst withstand ye three in any venture that might chance. Now hath my lady the queen taken counsel, and sent messengers far and near into every land to seek ye and Lancelot in this her sore need. And I be one of these messengers, and have ridden as swiftly as my steed might bear me from Arthur's Court hitherward, and ever have I sought tidings of ye, till at length men told me, and I knew that ye twain had come over to this cross, to this parting of the ways. And beyond the border did men tell me that would I ride hither I must fare for long upon the road ere I found a soul, man or woman, who lived, and was of the faith of Christendom. Against this did I prepare myself, and brought with me food, meat and bread, lest I had need thereof, and cool clear wine in two flasks that hang here by my saddle, that I might lay my hand on them when I had need thereto."

Then laughed Sir Gawain the bold when he heard him speak of food, and said that he had come thither in a good hour since they had no victuals, much or little, nor drink there within, nor knew they where they might find any had he brought none with him. But God had thought upon them betimes, and Mary, His Blessed Mother.

Then quoth Sir Gariët his brother, "Let us eat and drink, and begin our meal, as we have need to do—but where is Sir Lancelot, that I see him not here? Sir Gawain, brother, tell me, for fain would I know the truth?"

And Sir Gawain spake, "He rode hence a while ago to seek Sir Perceval."

Sir Gariët answered and said, "That ye vex yourselves thus to seek him, 'tis labour lost, for tidings have come to court that Perceval hath become hermit, and doeth penance for his sins. He hath learnt the truth; did he seek till Doomsday that which he went forth to seek, the spear and the grail, he would find them not; that cometh altogether from his sin against his mother whereas he left her in the forest, and would no more remain with women—then did she die for sorrow. That sin hath hindered him, did he otherwise come upon them, of winning the spear and the grail. He must be pure and clean from all stain, from all sin (so is it now declared for truth) who would have the spear at his will, and the grail. For sorrow at this hath Perceval betaken himself to a hermitage, thereof have tidings come to court, even as he willed that it should be made known. And concerning his brother Sir Agloval, of him did they tell that he lay sick, with his uncle, sorely wounded; but the messenger did us to wit that he was like to be healed, that do I tell ye, Sir Gawain. Now let us eat, and go on our way to the queen with honour, that doth my lady require of ye and of Sir Lancelot, upon your faith to her. But I am sore vexed that he hath thus escaped me!"

When Morien, the son of Sir Agloval, had heard and understood this tale, he asked forthwith if any there within could give him true tidings and make known to him the road to the hermitage whither his uncle had betaken himself, and where his father lay wounded; since he would fain know thereof.

Their host quoth straightway, "He that had a boat at his will and a favouring wind might be there ere even." He said that he knew the hermit; "And 'twixt water and land 'tis a good fifteen mile thither, that do I know for a truth, for oft-times have I heard men speak thereof since I came hither. Now hearken to what I tell ye," (thus he spake to Morien) "over the arm of the sea, there where ye cross, neither more nor less, on the further shore is there a forest, to all seeming the greatest men may wot of, and the wildest—'tis long withal and wide. But as ye come thither, to one side, at the entering in of the forest, they who would seek it may find the hermitage within but a short distance, even as it were the mountance of a mile. Of this be ye sure, with never a doubt."

"So help me God," quoth Morien, "an it fall out according to my will there shall I be ere even. And may I but see my father, an good luck befall me, I turn not from that goal, e'en if I find the man who gave me life, but ere I depart he shall keep the vow that he sware to my mother when he aforetime parted from her, and left her sorrowing sore, even that he would wed her, and make her his wife. Rather would I, ere even, be flayed with a sharp knife than refrain from this. Were he twofold my father he might well be in fear of death, should he fail to keep his oath, and ride with me to the Moorish land." He began to make ready as one who would straightway ride thence.

Then spake Sir Gariët, "An God will, it shall fall out better than ye say, 'twixt ye and your father; we will eat and drink, and I rede ye, an ye be wise, ye shall bethink ye well ere ye do aught save good to your father. I conjure ye by the faith that ye owe to our Lady, and by the honour of knighthood, that ye do my bidding, and let your thoughts be of good, and not of evil, and hearken Sir Gawain's rede, thereof shall never harm befall ye—he shall give ye the best counsel."

And Morien answered that were he fain to do.

Herewith they left speaking of this matter, and Sir Gariët brought forth a napkin, white and clean, and spread it before the knights, as is meet for noble folk, and those worthy of honour. Then he brought forth more than seven loaves, white as snow, that he had with him, and laid them upon the napkin before the knights. He brought forth ham and venison that he had bidden make ready, there, where he had lain over night, since that men told him he drew near to the wilderness whither had gone the knights whom he sought, and who rode before him. Since he was upon their track he had risen long ere 'twas day, and now came thither with the sun-rising. He brought forth also clear wine, two good bottles full. He was not altogether dull in that he had so well bethought him, and brought food with him lest peradventure he have need thereof. 'Twas right welcome to them who now partook of it; and through these good victuals forgat they all their tribulation, as they ate and drank. They were above measure joyful, those three knights, at that time, and with them the hermit, for they would in no wise forget him, but he must eat and drink with them.

When the meal was ended then Morien thought to ride on his way. But the good knight Sir Gariët said, "Sir Knight ye will do better to abide than to depart in this haste, in short while shall ye have trouble an ye seek your father. Follow ye our counsel; 'tis now high day, did ye come in safety to the ships it would be o'er late ere ye came to the other side."

Quoth Sir Gawain his brother, as one wise in counsel, "Knight I will tell ye what ye shall do; from haste cometh seldom good that abideth to honour. Therefore tarry over night with us, since ye may not achieve your goal this day; and I will make ready my weapons as best I may; I must needs be better healed ere I have strength to ride whither I would. Tomorrow shall it fare better with me. Then will we ride, without delay, so soon as it be daylight. If God will I shall be more at ease in limbs and at heart, and I shall have less pain than I have as at this while. I have no mind to abide here behind ye, nor to hinder ye and cause ye to delay when ye would fain ride hence, as I know right well! Here have I foes nigh at hand, who have wrought me harm, and were ready to do yet more did they know me to be here, in this place."

Then did Morien after his counsel, and abode there throughout the night, and told all the adventures that had befallen him. And Sir Gawain made ready his harness and his weapons, and scoured and polished them, and tested them where they were mishandled. But that which grieved him the most was his sorrow for his good sword which he had thus lost, for it was a sword of choice.

What boots it to make long my tale? The morrow as the day dawned, and shed beauty over hill and vale, they rode forth together, and Sir Gawain the Father of Adventure with them. They would not spare themselves. Then said Sir Gawain he would fare in quest of Sir Lancelot who departed with him from court when he left King Arthur, since he might not well, for his honour, return without him. He wist not how it had gone with him; and would fain learn how his venture had fallen out and return in short space, would God prosper him, and bring Sir Lancelot with him to the aid of the queen. On this was his mind set, nor would he do otherwise, for any man's prayer.

With this was Sir Gariët but ill-pleased; he said Sir Gawain would do better to return, and take the place of his uncle, and care for the land and comfort the folk. But this he would not do, howsoe'er he prayed him, but said he must first seek Sir Lancelot, and learn if harm had befallen him. Sir Gariët gave him his sword, which was good and bright; then took they leave, each of the other, for Sir Gawain would not return ere he had spoken with Sir Lancelot, saying that the good fellowship betwixt them twain should not be broken by his default; but that he would bring him again to the court of King Arthur, and keep his covenant.

When they were thus made ready, armed and fittingly clad, they mounted their steeds as they who would ride on their way. They took leave of the good man, their host, and departed thence.

Sir Gawain had chosen his road, and Sir Gariët and Sir Morien bare him company for a space, as it were the mountance of a mile. Each spake his mind to the other. Sir Gawain said he would return with Sir Lancelot as swiftly as he might, and put to shame the folk who had led his uncle captive; and he quoth, "Brother, tell this to my lady the queen, and bear her greeting in all good faith and loyalty. 'Tis not my will that ye ride further, nor tarry longer with me, since 'twill profit ye naught!"

Then Sir Gariët and Sir Morien turned their bridle. They commended Sir Gawain to the care of God and all His saints, and so did he them. Each saw the other's tears spring from their eyes and run down even to their beards when they parted asunder. I may not tell ye how oft and how warmly Sir Gawain thanked Morien, that he had saved his life that day on the field, where he had of a surety been slain had not God and that good knight come to his aid. Now will I here cease speaking of Sir Gawain and tell of Sir Morien. The adventure doeth us to wit that when Sir Morien and Sir Gariët had parted from Sir Gawain, they rode once more to the crossways, for they had made a compact that they should not part before that they had found his father, Sir Agloval. Thus they rode both together, for Morien sware an oath that, would Sir Gariët ride with him, he would e'en pray his uncle and his father to come to the aid of the queen, King Arthur's wife, and help her to win back her land. On this covenant and on this behest would Sir Gariët ride with him and bear Morien company.

As they came to the ships, Morien told him how it had fared with him before when he thought to make the crossing, and he said that he found no living soul among all that he saw there who would let him into his ship, since he seemed to them so huge, and black withal.

"They counted themselves for lost, deeming that I were the devil, and were sore afeard, and put out to sea. Now see, Sir Gariët, what counsel ye may find, and how we may so contrive that we cross the water; doubt ye not that an they once behold me and know me they will straightway set sail again and put to sea. I fear me we may not cross over!"

Quoth Sir Gariët: "By what ye tell me, methinks 'twere better that I ride on ahead, and hire me a ship. Ye shall follow on softly; and let me once come therein, and have my steed aboard and the boatman in my power, he shall not depart hence ere that ye be come thither. May my soul be lost if he do!" Further spake the knight Sir Gariët: "Even should he be beside himself when he first see ye, I shall not let him free ere he have taken us to the further shore, or I shall have from him such forfeit 'twere better for him to be sunken and drowned in the depths of the sea!"

Then answered Morien: "Ye have found the best counsel that may be devised. Now ride ye without delay, and hire us a boat, good and strong, that may well carry us over the water. I shall abide behind, and wait till ye have done your part. I will do even as ye shall counsel!"

Thus they agreed together, and Sir Gariët rode alone till he came to the ships, where he found a boat that pleased him well. He offered the boatman money enow to take him to the further side with no delay. He gave him the gold in his hand, and he made him ready and hoisted sail and rigging. Of this did he swiftly repent. Even as the steed was aboard and all was ready for the crossing came Morien riding, blacker than any son of man whom Christian eyes had e'er beheld. And the boatman was fain to flee when he beheld him and he drew nigh to him, for he had seen him aforetime. He deemed that he should surely die of fear, and scarce might move a limb.

Then Sir Gariët asked him: "Sir boatman, what aileth thee? By Heaven, it availeth thee naught; thou shall ferry us over swiftly. Now make us no ado, or this shall be thy last day. By the Lord who made us, of what art thou afraid? This is not the devil! Hell hath he never seen! 'Tis but my comrade; let him in. I counsel thee straitly!"

Then must the boatman obey, though he liked it but ill. He saw that better might not be: he might neither leap out of the boat nor otherwise escape. So soon as he had in his boat Morien, of whom he was sore afraid, in that he was so huge, and had shipped his steed, which was in seeming over-strong, he pushed the boat from shore and put out to sea. He feared him greatly, even as one who deems that he is lost.

When Morien had sat himself down he did off his helmet of steel. Then the boatman deemed that he was a dead man, and prayed for mercy, beholding his face, for he though he might scarce be a Christian. Sir Gariët asked of him tidings, if there had passed that way two knights, of whom the one bestrode a red horse and wore red armour, and the other bare the badge of King Arthur. If he might tell him aught of them he besought him to do so; an he knew where they yet abode he would give him great thanks.

The boatman said: "'Tis not long since that they were even in my boat; the one knight ware red armour and had with him a red steed, and the other was wounded and bare King Arthur's badge; and I know full well," quoth the boatman, "the knights who bear that badge, by that same token shall ye yourself be one of King

Arthur's knights. They would both cross over, and I ferried them to the further side. 'Twas to them an unknown land; that did I hear well from their speech. Methought that they were ill at ease, I wist not wherefore. I saw that the one wept so that the tears fell thick adown his face. And when I had brought them to the other side the knight, who was glad thereof, asked me if I knew where stood a hermitage wherein a hermit dwelt. That did I shew him—no more and no less."

Thus fared they, having heard the tale and speaking of the twain, till that they touched the sand. Then did the boatman shew them the way they should ride thence to where the hermitage stood, and declared to them the road. Thus left they the boatman, who was much rejoiced to be safely quit of them. But the knights went on their way till they knew that they drew near to the hermitage, and came even unto it. Then they dismounted, and made fast their steeds before the door, and cried with a loud voice to those within: "Let us in! Open of your goodwill!" A lad came to the door and asked them what they desired, and if aught ailed them that they required aid.

Then Sir Gariët spake, and said that an it were pleasing to them, they would fain have speech with the hermit and with Sir Agloval. And the messenger went his way to the twain, and told them how two knights stood without the gate. "The one is a goodly man to look upon and well armed, and so, forsooth, is the other, but his armour and his limbs, so far as I might see, were blacker than soot or pitch. I wot not if ye know aught of them or of their errand. They said that they would fain speak with ye, and they prayed me straitly, the twain of them, that I should come hither and tell ye this."

Sir Agloval, who deemed this passing strange, went, as best he might, to the gate, and his uncle the hermit followed him with no delay. Sir Agloval looked through the wicket, and was ware of Sir Gariët, Sir Gawain's brother, and bethought him how that he belonged to King Arthur's court and was worthy of great honour, for though he were not so well known throughout the land as was his brother Sir Gawain, yet was he a strong knight and bold, and a doer of valiant deeds.

When they beheld each other they gave fair and courteous

greeting, the one to the other, and Sir Gariët spake. "May He who can do all things shew favour and honour to ye Sir Knight, and to all who be with ye there within!"

Sir Agloval looked upon Morien, and marked right well the fashion of him, and marvelled within himself what manner of knight he might well be who bare such guise. And Morien stood before him and asked him if he yet remembered how, seeking for Sir Lancelot, he came into the land of the Moors, and how he there loved a maiden, and plighted to her his troth, and how she granted to him her favours ere he departed from her upon his quest. He asked him if he yet thought thereupon, how, when he departed from the land he pledged his word to her that he would return, so soon as might be, to the country of the Moors, for her profit and for her honour? Did he yet think upon this?

Sir Agloval made answer: "Sir Knight, I make no denial, yet have I but seldom been at rest. I rode in quest of Sir Lancelot awhile; and thereafter had I but little respite, since I brought my brother to court, where he was held in high honour, and so soon as he was made knight must I ride forth with him upon a journey which he would in no wise delay; for he was fain to avenge the harm done to our father many a year agone—that must ye understand. My brother knew well that our foes had taken to themselves the heritage that should have been ours, when they drave my father forth. This would he avenge, and spare not, and herein had we much strife ere we might regain it; but now have we done so much that we have won back our heritage and slain all those who had possessed themselves of our land. That so many years have fled since I sware to the maiden that I would return to her, that came of necessity. Now have I failed to keep mine oath, and needs must that I bethink me well, and seek counsel in the matter. I know not, and have no true tidings, whether that lady of whom ye speak be living or dead; naught do I know thereof!"

Quoth Morien: "But I shall tell ye more thereof! She to whom ye gave your troth yet liveth and is my mother, and ye, Sir Knight, are my father! If ye will come with me, at her prayer and mine, then will ye do well and courteously. Ye begat me upon her who should be your wife, had ye kept your oath. Now bethink ye well, and say if ye will come or no. When ye parted from my mother she bare me though she knew it not. Thus, Sir Knight, did the matter fall out."

Sir Agloval made answer: "By Heaven Sir Knight, I believe ye, every whit. That which the lady claimeth from me, in that I have thus betrayed her and foresworn mine oath, that will I make good, by the help of God. I will yet win her grace. Come ye to me here within to mine uncle and my brother, they shall counsel us well when they hear our tale—so shall we be more at ease."

With that he undid the wicket. 'Twould have done any heart good, who understood their speech, to see how Sir Agloval and Morien embraced and kissed each other. Any heart would have been the gladder who had seen and heard their gestures and their words, and in what love and friendship they betook themselves within, where they were right well received. Sir Agloval forthwith made known to his uncle and to Sir Perceval the true tale of his doings, and how that his son had come hither.

When Sir Perceval heard this, never did knight receive so glad a welcome as that which he gave unto his nephew; so likewise did the hermit. 'Twas bliss and fair speech there betwixt those knights, and in their honour did they bring forth such food and drink as was there within, and did all they might for their comfort. That even was there naught but gladness; each made great joy of the other, and erst as the knights were weary did they get them to sleep, as men are wont to do, till the day brake, and the sun shone forth.

The knights lay longer abed than did the hermit, who had said and sung his orisons and his Mass ere day had dawned, or that the knights had arisen and done on their garments. Then spake Morien to his father, even as ye shall hear, and said he would ride thence, and was fain to know, without contention, if he would come with him to his mother, and do that which he promised when he departed from her, for the sake of God and of his own honour, and for their profit. He told how they had been deprived of their rightful heritage which had fallen to his mother from her father. "'Twas altogether denied her by the law of the land; yet 'twas the shame rather than the loss that grieved her, in that men called her son fatherless, and she might bring no proof of her word, nor shew them to their face the man who had begotten me!"

Then said Sir Agloval, his father: "I will tell ye out and out how the thing stands with me, and tell ye all my counsel. Believe me well, I will not lie to ye in one word." And Morien hearkened and answered that he believed him fully.

Thus they abode that day with the hermit, and were better served, in all that men might prepare for them, than I may well tell ye; and Morien prayed his father straitly that he would delay not, but would tell him what was in his thought and in his intent. Thus did he urge his father, till Sir Agloval told him all his mind.

He said that he beheld a vision in a dream; it seemed to him that he rode throughout the day in a land where he saw naught but wilderness and wood, and trees, many and fair. By whiles he rode through hail and snow, by whiles through noontide heat, so that he was sore vexed. Whiles he saw the sun shine bright, whiles it was as if the twilight fell. He saw all kinds of beasts run through the forest, and folk, young and old, go up and down the woods. All this did he see in his dream, but nowhere in all this land did he come to where he might find shelter. But as it drew towards evening, and the light failed, did he think to see a tower, so strongly built that none by force might lightly win their way within; but no doorway might he see, only, as it were, another tower that stood there. Within this he beheld a stairway, that wound upward to a doorway at the end. The door seemed to him high as a church, and of wrought ironwork. Were a man sick he might well be healed by the light that streamed forth from within, for, as he saw and looked upon it, it seemed as it might well be Heaven. And every step of the stairway was of good red gold. And he thought within himself that since those steps were so fair he might well set foot thereon, and tell the tale of them, how many they might be, that hereafter he might speak of the great marvel he had seen. But as he had counted sixty, and would set foot upon the next, lo! he saw none of all those he had left below him, save that upon which he stood, and on which his foot was set, and above him he saw naught. And it seemed to him that the door was distant from the step as high as one might shoot with a bow. Thus might he go neither forward nor backward. Then he beheld, and on the ground beneath were serpents and wild bears, even as if they would tear him; they gnashed their teeth as if they would seize him, and gaped with their jaws as they would swallow him. It seemed to him as if they were even at his heels, and he saw the snakes and dragons all twist themselves upwards. "And as I was thus fearful the step brake beneath me, and I fell downwards." From his great discomfort and his fear of the dragons he awoke, and slept no more.

The dream vexed him sorely whenever he thought thereon; he was angry and wroth, and wist not what the portent of the vision might be. But his heart forbode him that pain and mischief, and sore labour withal, drew nigh to him. Then it fell out that he met with a learned clerk, to whom he told the vision even as it had appeared to him; and when he had hearkened to his tale, and understood it well, he interpreted it in this wise: "Concerning our lands, great and small, that we thereof should be in great stress and fear ere we might win to them again; for strong were the castles and mighty the armies, therefore did the vision foretell ill to my brother and myself each and singly. And further he spake concerning my brother Perceval, and the Spear, and the Grail; for that golden stairway betokened the Holy Grail, and that Perceval should aid in the winning thereof, and in that service should he die. Thus did he foretell me. And the door that stood above and the stairway itself both alike betokened the heavenly kingdom, as might well be known by the light that shone within; and the steps that lay before it they betokened the days of Perceval's life. 'This I tell ye of a truth, each betokeneth a day, or a week, or it may be a month; but of this be ye sure, and doubt not, so long shall he live, and then shall he yield up his life. And that the steps brake beneath ye, 'twas for your sins; ye had well-nigh climbed them had not sin laid hold on ye. The bears, and the dragons, and the serpents that there lay in wait, know ye well that they gave sure and certain sign that the fiends deemed they had ye for their own in that hour, and would carry ye to Hell.'" Thus did the wise master make known to him his dream, and bade him thereof take warning and order his ways with wisdom, and that speedily, and delay not, for here should he abide no long time, but drew nigh to his end.

"Dear son," quoth Sir Agloval, "then did my brother cease his quest for the Spear and the Grail, and the adventure on which he was bound, and came hither as swiftly as he might to mine uncle the hermit, and clothed himself in this habit, through that which the clerk foretold me. Thus are we here together, and my brother would fain amend his life. Nor am I yet whole; for I was wounded wellnigh to death, and bruised and mishandled, so that I had no power left, and am yet scarce healed. Thus would I abide here awhile with my brother and mine uncle, that my wounds might be tended, and that with them I might save my soul. Now ye will that I journey with ye to your mother in the Moorish land, and I were fain to ride thither were I but healed. Yet is there another matter. I would gladly go with ye, that may ye know of a truth, for your honour, and to do away your shame, were it not that I thus brought about my death; nevertheless, I have trust in mine uncle, who is so wise, that he shall make my peace with God, and bring me to eternal bliss. Now, son, bethink ye of our profit, yours and mine, according to that which has befallen me, and that ye have now heard even as I tell ye. Counsel me as it seemeth ye best; since that I be your father, according as matters went afore 'twixt me and your mother, it behoves ye well so to do."

Then quoth Morien: "Were ye better healed I would ride gladly, but it becometh me well to shun aught that might do ye harm or mischief. I can give ye none other counsel than that ye abide here till ye be once more whole. King Arthur is captive and his land is beset and in sore stress. Here is his nephew Sir Gariët, who hath come hither with me, and now that I have learnt the truth I shall ride with him to court, to do him honour, and there abide till that ye be whole and healed; and I will return hither in the hour that I know ye be cured of your wounds and may keep the oath that ye sware to my mother, that ye be praised of men and in favour with God. So shall my mother once more be possessed of the lands of which she hath been disinherited, and which she hath this long time lacked. I shall depart and ye shall abide here, where may all good befall ye! I will aid the queen, and God grant that I may win such fame as shall be for the bettering of her cause and mine own honour and profit. I shall return, be ye sure of it, when the time is ripe, and shall ever think of ye as my father."

Then all thanked Morien, deeming that as at that time no better counsel might be found; and Sir Gariët and Morien alike besought of Sir Perceval that he would ride with them, to aid the queen and release King Arthur, and bring comfort to his land. This he sware to do would his uncle grant him leave thereto. Then did they all, and Sir Agloval with them, so straitly pray the uncle that he granted their request, and never might ye see at any time folk so blithe as were these knights in that Sir Perceval would ride with them. Thus did they take their leave and wend on their way. But now will I leave speaking of them and tell how it fared with Sir Lancelot, who would slay the evil beast.

Now doth the adventure tell us that when Sir Lancelot departed from Sir Gawain at the cross-roads he delayed not, but rode that same hour till he came to the waste land wherein the beast had wrought havoc. Now in that land there dwelt a maiden who had caused it to be made known far and wide that whosoever might slay that beast him would she take for her husband. Never might man behold a fairer maiden, and the land was all in her own power. Now there dwelt also therein a traitor, a knight who loved the maiden, but had little mind to risk his life for her; he kept close watch upon that beast if so be that any man should slay it that he might play the traitor, so should the slayer pay with his life for the deed, and he should spread abroad that he himself had, of a verity, slain the monster.

Thus Sir Lancelot rode so far into the land that he came nigh to the place where he had heard that the fearful beast had made its lair. There did he see many a helm, and spear, and weapon of the knights it had slain, whose bones lay there stripped of flesh, which the monster had devoured; he might well be afraid! So soon as Lancelot might know where the beast was wont to lie, he made haste thitherward, and so soon as it was ware of his coming it came flying in such guise as it had been the Devil, and set upon Sir Lancelot straightway. It feared neither sword nor spear, nor armour, nor might of man. And Lancelot smote at the monster so that his spear brake in twain, yet had he not bruised it a whit, or pierced its hide; then he drew forth his sword and smote with great force, but he harmed it not, and it seized Lancelot by the throat and scored him in such wise that the knight was wroth thereof, for it tare a great rent through the hauberk even to the flesh, and wounded him sore. Many a time did Sir Lancelot strike and smite at the beast, but never a groat might he harm it; but the monster fell upon Sir Lancelot and scored him even to the feet, and dealt him many a wound, and breathed out venom upon him; had it not been for a ring which Sir Lancelot ware upon his finger he had fallen dead where he stood from the poison. Then the monster sprang towards him with gaping jaws, as it were fain to swallow him, and Lancelot watched his chance, and thrust his sword into its mouth, and clave the heart in sunder, and the beast gave a cry so terrible that 'twas heard a good two mile off.

Then the traitor who spied all from afar, when he heard the cry delayed not, but rode swiftly towards the lair, for he knew well from the cry that the monster was slain. When he came to the place he found Sir Lancelot sitting, binding up his wounds, which were many and deep. The knight began to bemoan his plight, and went towards him saying that he would bind his wounds for him. That cowardly and wicked knight, he came even to Sir Lancelot's side, and snatched stealthily at his sword, and sprang backward and smote at him, wounding him so that he fell as one dead.

When the false traitor saw this he deemed that he was dead, and left him lying, and went there, where the monster lay, and smote off the right foot, thinking to take it to the maiden of whom I have told ye, that he might therewith win her to wife.

But in this while had Sir Gawain ridden so far that he had learned the truth how that Sir Lancelot had found the beast, and at this time he had followed upon his tracks and came unto the lair even as the traitor had wounded Sir Lancelot, and cut off the foot, and was mounted upon Sir Lancelot's steed, which that good knight, Sir Gawain, knew right well.

So soon as he saw the stranger upon the steed, and Lancelot, who lay there wounded, he rode fast towards him, and drew out his good sword, and cried, "Abide ye still, Sir Murderer, for this beast have ye slain my comrade, that do I see right well." That false and cruel knight had fain ridden thence, but Sir Gawain was so nigh to him that he could not avoid, and smote at him so fiercely that he must needs abide, and draw bridle, and pray for mercy.

Sir Gawain was of a mind to bring him to Sir Lancelot ere he made terms with him. Thus they came together, and Lancelot, who was now recovered from the swoon in which he had lain, and was ware of Sir Gawain, cried to him concerning the traitor who had smitten him all unarmed, "Dear comrade, slay him. I shall die the easier, knowing that he be already dead." As he spake thus, Sir Gawain made no more ado but smote off the traitor's head.

Then did he forthwith go to bemoan his comrade, and quoth, "Sir Knight, may ye not be healed? Tell me now the truth; I will aid ye as I may." Then Sir Lancelot did him to wit how he had fared with the beast, and how the traitor had thereafter wounded him. "And this hath wrought me the greater harm; yet might I but find a place wherein to rest methinks I might well be healed."

Then was Sir Gawain glad at heart, and he bound up his wounds forthwith with herbs of such virtue as should stay the bleeding; and he took Sir Lancelot and set him upon his steed, and turned him again towards the hermit's cell as best he might, for 'twas in both their minds that might they but come thither Sir Gawain should surely heal him. Thus did they ride until they had found the hermitage, and scarce had they come thither when they were ware of Morien with Sir Gariët and Sir Perceval, who came thither as at that time.

Then was there joy and gladness manifold. The Hermit made ready food for his guests, and prepared a couch for Sir Lancelot as best he might. Each told the other how matters had fallen out with them, and Morien gave them to wit how it had fared with his father.

That night were they well entreated by the hermit, but the morrow so soon as Sir Lancelot heard how it went with the queen, even should he gain the world thereby he had remained no longer, neither for wounds nor for weariness, for, he said, he was surely healed, and was fain to be at strife. Thus must they all ride forth, whether they would or no, with the early morning, for they might not lose a day. Sir Gawain would tend Sir Lancelot's wounds even as they rode on their way.

Thus they journeyed till they heard true tidings of their lady, the queen; how that she was beset on all sides by the King of Ireland. He had burnt and laid waste so much men scarce knew the tale thereof, and the queen had he beset in a castle to which he himself laid siege. For he had sworn a great oath, nor would he lightly break it, that might he win the castle he should spare no man of all that were within, but should put such shame upon them, and on the queen, that men should speak thereof for all time. Thus had the king sworn by his crown, and by all that may bind a king, that he would do them bitter shame.

When the knights of whom I tell ye came into Arthur's land they saw there a castle, around which ran a swift water, broad and deep. He who builded that burg was well counselled. The castle was of grey hewn stone. King Arthur had never a stronghold in the losing of which he had lost so much, and this was not yet lost. But the folk that were within had no more than a day's grace left to them, on the morrow must they fare forth, for would they defend it no quarter should be shown them, but they should be seethed or roasted alive. This had the king sworn and on the morrow would he come thither; he had laid waste the country and destroyed the churches, and made many widows and orphans; all the land was in terror for the harm thus wrought upon them. The knights who came thither saw the folk as they fled with all their goods and their foodstuff, they deemed theirs was a lost cause. They met many folk, men women and children who would flee the land; they drave their cattle before them and were laden with their goods; some were ahorse, some afoot, 'twas the best they might do to their thinking.

Then Sir Gariët gave courteous greeting to one whom he met, and asked who were this folk, and wherefore they fled thus in haste? And the goodman answered straight-way: "They deem that all is lost; the King cometh hither to this castle that standeth here, and the people of the land know not what they may do, they must lose their goods and all they possess. Here hath a great misfortune chanced, the ordeal hath gone over us; King Arthur hath been taken captive and we know not where he may be, he was waylaid and betrayed in a forest, whither he went to hunt, and we saw him never more. The King of Ireland hath seized upon all this land, he who would save his life must perforce yield to him, for he hath with him a mighty army and our folk are defenceless. We lack leaders—Sir Gawain and Sir Lancelot have both of them left the land, and thereof hath great shame come to us—we are without king, or leaders, or counsel."

Quoth Morien: "This castle that standeth here, is there yet any man within?"

The goodman said: "I tell ye there are ten knights within (and they have naught but death before them), and a great company of foot soldiers. Now must they reap that mischance which hath fallen upon the land. They might well have held the castle for a year to come, so strong is it, and they have within weapons and victuals, and men enough for the defence—it might scarce be taken by force so long as they had food, nor might any man lightly make his way therein. But methinks God hath forsaken us. The king hath sworn an oath that if need be he will besiege the castle seven years, and all they who withstand him, and whom he shall find within at his coming thither, shall lose their lives; this hath he made known to them. And their wives and their children, though their lives be spared, shall be deprived of their goods and their heritage. Thus, since we may not hope for aid, we are forsaking the castle and taking to flight."

Quoth Sir Gawain: "Good friend, God reward ye for your tidings."

Then Sir Gawain bethought him that 'twere best they rode within the castle which was a fair burg, and strong; and that they should there greet the knights and strangers who might be within, bidding them trust in God that He would bring their matter to a good ending. The knights were right well received, for all knew them well, and made great rejoicing over the coming of Sir Gawain and Sir Lancelot. Then did Sir Gawain give them to wit of the good knight Sir Morien, what he had done for them, and how he was one of the best knights the sun ever shone upon. Thus spake Sir Gawain.

Then said Sir Morien: "'Tis good that we abide here within, and brave the venture for the sake of the king our lord. 'Twere a sin and a disgrace to yield up the castle, we should better adventure our lives and see the matter to an end."

Sir Gawain and Sir Lancelot took up the word and said: "He who faileth his king 'tis right that men speak shame of him thereafter throughout the world. Would ye have good fortune ye must await what cometh, and I have good hope that heaven shall shortly send us help. Here may we well win fame for ourselves and uphold the honour of our lord King Arthur. Though he be now a captive yet, an God will, he shall escape. My heart and my mind fore-tell me that will we but hold out here within it shall be to our honour!"

Thus did Sir Gawain and Sir Lancelot admonish them, even as I tell ye, and when they had hearkened to their words those who were within, and had thought to depart, when they knew what was the mind of those knights, sware that never a knight nor squire, nor man-at-arms would give himself up, or forsake that good castle. Morien's counsel seemed to them good, and although he were not fair to look upon yet when he stood upon his feet it seemed to them that had he the chance he might put to the rout a whole army! Each man there gave his surety to abide with them at that time, nor to surrender through fear of death, but to hearken to other counsel.

When all had sworn the oath, and given surety, then did they shut fast the portals upon all their food and all the aid they might win against the king and his army who were nigh at hand.

Ere the day darkened came the king himself, in great wrath, and with him many knights who belonged to his household, and many other folk, warlike to behold, and came even to the castle. Then the king demanded of those who were within if they would yield up the burg, and thus save their lives. And they within answered that so long as life remained to them they would not give up the castle, or betray their rightful lord. Then swore the king an oath that an they yielded them not up straight-way they should in no wise escape the uttermost that he might do unto them. But for that they cared little, and made them ready for the defence. They thought to remain upon the battlements, and throw from the castle stones so great and so heavy that the king should be driven from the walls out on to the open field where he had pitched his tents.

With that had the night fallen, and they who had come into the land set up tents and pavilions, and would lodge in the green-wood. When they of within saw that they took counsel together, and said did they leave them in peace that night the king would, doubtless, send for a greater force of knights and other folk, and assemble a mighty army, and it were better that they should now adventure themselves, and ride forth from the castle ere they were yet more outnumbered. Hereof had they bethought them ere yet they came to counsel.

Sir Lancelot spake thus: "Flee we may not, nor dare we hope for aid, nor may we surrender the castle; in this way shall we profit better." Thus were they that night within the castle, neither with game nor with revel, but they held together as true knights and good comrades. They ate and drank of such victuals as they had, and never a man of them wavered as it drew nigh to the dawning; they were fain to do great deeds; each looked to his armour as one who will fight for his life, and gave his steed a feed of corn.

What boots it to make long my tale? With the dawning of the day were they of within ready, each man well armed and mounted on a good steed. They rode out betimes, and bade undo the gates. Thus did they ride forth in all their strength.

They who kept shield-watch without were ware of them, and led their company against them, but it harmed them naught. Morien's weapons were so strong; 'twas he led the vanguard, nor would he yield an inch when he began the strife. Never might one behold mortal man who smote such strokes. They fought their way through that camp. Sir Gawain, Sir Perceval, and Sir Lancelot smote many to death, and came even to the king's tents, and seized their weapons, shields, and spears, ere his folk might come at their arms. They knew not what had befallen them. No quarter would the knights give. They who were with the king slept sound in their ranks, and were sore afeard when they awoke and beheld the armed men who beset them with stern intent; they had many a sore wound ere they fled from the field.

They took the king by main force; there was no man at his side but was glad and blithe might he escape with his life. The king must yield himself a prisoner, thereto did need compel him, otherwise had he been slain and all his folk with him.

They led the king within the castle, and shut him fast in a tower. Never had they so welcome a guest, nor one at whose coming they were so blithe. They on the field must escape as best they might. Little did they reck of all they brought with them; he might win it who had a mind thereto. When the fight was ended King Arthur's men had taken captive much folk and the King of Ireland. Matters had gone well for them. They held there within that which they deemed many would buy dearly, nor count the gold therefor, nor might they well tell how they had lost it. But 'twas their dread of Morien's mighty blows, and of Sir Lancelot, Sir Gawain, and Sir Perceval, who, on the field, had brought many in sore terror and dread of death.

So brought they their guests within the walls, and shut fast their gates, and hung out their shields, as men who might well defend themselves. Then when men beheld Sir Gawain's badge, and Sir Lancelot's pennon beside it, tidings of the combat ran far and wide through the land. The king's folk who lay there were sore vexed thereat. So soon as they who had besieged the queen heard what had chanced they drew off their forces; and all they who served the king, and who came with him into the lands, were greatly shamed, and desired of Sir Gawain in what wise they might make peace.

Sir Gawain took counsel with his comrades, and this was their rede, that they must bring King Arthur there before their eyes ere they might make terms for their lord, the king. "Then shall we have such good counsel on all points that peace may thereby be made."

Wherefore should I make my tale over long? Little as they liked it they must needs bring King Arthur thither, and thereby make terms for the king, their lord. When the tidings ran through the land that the King of Ireland was captive, and that King Arthur was brought thither to treat with him, then was there so great a gathering of Britons that they surrounded Arthur, and took him from the men of Ireland, and brought him with armed hand into the castle despite them all. Thus did it fall out well for King Arthur, since he thus escaped, and held captive the king who had erstwhile made him a prisoner.

Now shall ye hear of the King of Ireland, who lay thus in the prison of the knights. When he heard and beheld with his eyes that King Arthur was in very deed free, then did he betake himself to him straight-way, and offered him goods and gold that he might be set at liberty, and he sware that he would be the king's man, and hold all his lands henceforward from him, and would depart from the kingdom with all his folk. Thus must the king, being captive, stand at King Arthur's pleasure to pay him such ransom as he might think good. Of him will I speak no more.

Now was King Arthur so blithe thereof that he bid hold a great court, that he might give largesse to all who desired. Thither came many, but none were there of such renown, or who had wrought such valiant deeds, as Sir Perceval and Morien. The reward that Arthur gave them was exceeding great. Sir Gawain told the king all the matter of Morien and of his father, and the chance that had parted them. All this did he tell afore the folk, wherefore was Morien much gazed upon. Now will I leave this tale and tell ye how Morien rode again to his father, whom he had left sick with his uncle, as I gave ye to wit afore.

The adventure maketh known that when the strife was ended, and Arthur's land once more at peace, Morien bethought him that he would make his father be wedded to the lady, his mother; and he prayed his uncle to journey with him if he would, and Sir Perceval was right willing thereto. Further, said Sir Gawain and Sir Lancelot, that they twain would ride with them for honour and for good fellowship. For this did Morien thank them much. Thus they departed and went their way towards the hermitage. They rode blithely in company, telling of many things that had chanced here and elsewhere, until they came to the seashore, where they took ship and crossed over; and when they had passed the water they came straightway to Perceval's uncle, who received them with right goodwill.

By this was Sir Agloval whole, who had been wounded, and Morien asked him straightway if he were rightly healed, and would now keep the oath which he had aforetime sworn unto his mother. Sir Agloval answered that he was whole and sound, and ready thereto. "The troth that I swear to your mother will I keep what time as it shall please ye. As God is my witness I be altogether ready to do this."

Quoth Sir Perceval, "Then wherefore delay? Your son is so good a knight, and stout a warrior, that ye may well thank heaven that ye begat him. Make you ready straightway, and we will fare with ye. Sir Gawain and Sir Lancelot be come hither in faith and good fellowship, and with us will they journey to the Moorish land."

Then was there no longer delaying, but they made them ready for the journey, and went their way with Sir Morien, who knew the road better than any man of them all. They rode so long that they came thither; and when they of the land heard tell how that Morien had brought his father with him they assembled themselves together, and some were for refusing them entry into the kingdom, since they would fain keep the heritage for themselves. But when Morien heard this he waxed so wrathful that he drew his sword and rode among them where there was the greatest press, and slew there fifteen of the nobles who were fain to deny him his inheritance.

When the others knew of this they came to him and besought his grace, and yielded to him all his heritage, and gave it into the hand of his mother, and became her men, to hold their lands henceforward from her. When this was done, and they had proclaimed her queen over all the kingdom of the Moors, then did they hold the bridal feast of Sir Agloval and the queen, and thus were they wedded to each other. There was bliss and great rejoicing fourteen days, even till nightfall did they hold high feast with open doors; never a portal was shut. There was feasting and great merriment; there were all well served with everything on earth that they might desire. Many rich gifts were given, good steeds, raiment of fair colours, many shillings, many pounds, great plenty of all things by which men may the more blithely live. The minstrels and the heralds received great largesse, for there was gold enow; each had that which he desired.

There would Sir Gawain and Sir Lancelot abide till that the feast was ended; be ye sure that Sir Perceval and Sir Agloval the bridegroom prayed them thus to honour the bridal, and this they did, in right courteous wise. No man of them all, were he poor or rich, but had enough and to spare.

What more shall I say hereof? When the feast was ended, and all the nobles departed, and all had taken leave, then was it in the mind of Sir Gawain, Sir Lancelot, and Sir Perceval to betake them straightway to King Arthur's court, for 'twas nigh to Pentecost, and the king (thus do I read the tale) would hold high court (greater was never held) on behalf of Galahad, Sir Lancelot's son, for that this hero should then come to court, and receive the honour of knighthood. And thereof did the tale wax great; how that he should achieve the quest of the Grail, and all the adventures, small and great, which appertained to the Round Table, for 'twas said that he should sit in the Perilous Seat, wherein durst never man sit. To behold these marvels would many a man come to court, for the king had bidden all the great folk of the land thither, and many a knight of praise had obeyed his command.

And for this cause would not Sir Lancelot and Sir Gawain and Sir Perceval remain afar, but took their leave of Sir Agloval and of Morien and of his mother, and rode on their way till they came to King Arthur at Camelot, where he abode, as it pleased him well to do when he would fain be at peace. And when the king heard of the coming of these three knights, then was he right joyful at that time; and when he learnt concerning Sir Agloval, how his wedding feast had been held, and of the valiant deeds that Morien had done in his own land, then were king and queen alike glad at heart.

Here will I leave this tale and speak further concerning the Grail, and the winning thereof. That shall ye find set forth in the book that followeth hereafter; the other part, that which concerneth Lancelot, here cometh to an end. Now do I pray God in words straitly, that He have mercy upon me when my life shall come to an end, and bring my soul to His heavenly kingdom. May He grant this my prayer!

AMEN.

# NOTES

1. INTRODUCTION.—In the preface I have dwelt with some fulness on the interesting questions connected with these opening lines; here it will be sufficient to point out that in the earlier versions of the *Perceval* story the hero is either the only, or the sole surviving, son of his parents. The introduction of a brother, as a definite character, belongs to the later stages of Arthurian tradition. The brothers vary in number and name, but the most noted are Sir Agloval and Sir Lamorak, who appear to belong to distinct lines of development, Sir Agloval belonging mainly to the *Lancelot*, Sir Lamorak to the *Tristan* tradition. So far I have not met with the latter in any version of the prose *Lancelot*, though Dr. Sommer in his *Studies on the Sources of Malory*, refers to him as mentioned in that romance; in the *Tristan*, on the contrary, he is a leading figure. The *Morien* story, as I have remarked in the preface, has obviously been modified by the influence of the later *Lancelot* legend, hence, probably, the *rôle* assigned to Agloval.

2. PAGE 9.—*Gawain as physician.* The representation of Gawain as an expert in medical skill is an interesting feature which appears to belong to early tradition. The references in the poem before us are the most copious and explicit, but we also find the same accomplishment referred to in the romance of *Lancelot et le cerf au pied blanc* (D. L. vol. ii. 1. 22825) where Gawain instructs the physician as to the proper treatment of Lancelot's wounds; and the *Parzival* of Wolfram von Eschenbach (Book X. 1. 104) also refers to this tradition. It is noticeable that Chrétien de Troyes in the parallel passage of his poem has no such allusion, nor can I recall any passage in the works of that poet which indicates any knowledge, on his part, of this characteristic of Gawain. This is one of the points of variance between Chrétien and Wolfram which, slight in itself, offers when examined valuable evidence as to a difference of sources.

3. PAGE 11.—*The boast of Sir Kay.* Arthur's reproof to Kay is a reference to the well-known adventure related both by Chrétien and Wolfram and found moreover in the *Peredur*. The hero, thrown into a love-trance by the sight of blood-drops on the snow, gives no answer to the challenge addressed to him

successively by Segramore and Kay, and being rudely attacked by these knights overthrows them both. The allusion to this incident, which is not related in the prose *Lancelot*, shows clearly that while, on the whole, he is harmonising his romance with the indications of the later traditions, the writer is yet quite conversant with the earlier forms.

4. Page 12.— *The Father of Adventure.* "Der Aventuren Fader." The Middle English poem of *Sir Gawain and the Green Knight* (No. 1 of this Series) speaks of the knight in somewhat similar terms as "the fine father of courtesy." Gawain was from the first the adventurous hero, *par excellence* of the cycle, but I know no other instance in which this characteristic is so quaintly and forcibly expressed.

5. Page 13.—*In secret case.* The original words are "in hemeliker stede." To which particular adventure of Lancelot this refers it is not easy to decide; on more than one occasion he disappears from court, and the knights headed by Gawain, ride in quest of him. Perhaps this refers to his imprisonment by Morgain le Fay (*cf.* summary of *D.L.* in *Legend of Sir Lancelot du Lac.* Grimm's Library XII. pp. 236-7).

6. Page 17.—*Sir Agloval, he is my father.* This should be compared with the account of Gamuret's wooing and desertion of the Moorish queen, Belakane, in Book I. of the *Parzival*; also with the meeting of the unknown brothers in Book XV. of the same poem. It is perhaps worth noticing as indicative of the source of the tradition that Wolfram distinctly states that his Moor speaks in *French.*

7. Page 31-2,—*The slain and the slayer.* The belief that the blood of a corpse would flow afresh, did the murderer approach it, was very prevalent in the middle ages. In Chretien de Troyes' *Chevalier au lion* (ll. 1177 et seq.) we find a similar situation, complicated by the fact that Yvain (the slayer) protected by a magic ring is invisible to the bystanders. The best known instance, however, is probably that of the *Nibelungenlied* where Kriemhild's suspicions that Hagen is Siegfred's murderer are in this manner verified.

8. Page 43.—*I have no call to flee, nor to fear death.* This is evidently the hermit whom Lancelot in the *Queste* finds dead

under circumstances agreeing with those here hinted at. The story will be found in Malory Book XV.

9. PAGE 48.—*That cometh altogether from his sin against his mother.* The reason here alleged for Perceval's failure to find the Grail is that given by Chrétien and Wolfram, and is another indication of the writer's familiarity with the early *Perceval* story.

10. PAGE 55.—*Sir Agloval's explanation, (a) The Lancelot quest.* The special quest here referred to is that undertaken in search of Lancelot when he fled from court in a frenzy, induced by Guinevere's jealousy of King Pelles' daughter. During this quest Agloval visits his mother, sees Perceval, and brings him to court (*cf. Legend of Sir Lancelot* pp. 161-2).

*(b) The lost heritage.* The fact that Perceval regains possession of the heritage of which he has, before his birth, been deprived is recorded in certain of the *Perceval* romances; the *Parzival* of Wolfram von Eschenbach, the prose *Perceval li Gallois,* and the English *Sir Percyvelle of Galles,* but it is not found in Chrétien. It is clear, to a close observer, that the compiler of the Dutch *Lancelot* knew the early *Perceval* tradition in a form closer to the version of the German, than that of the French poet. Later on, in the *Queste* section, he introduces a reference to this inheritance, where none exists in the French versions I have examined (*cf. Legend of Sir Lancelot* p. 174).

11. PAGE 60.—*Lancelot's adventure with the beast.* This is a condensed account of the well known story of *The Fahe Claimant.* Two versions of this story have already been given in this series, the dragon adventure in *Tristan* (No. II) and that of the stag in *Tyolet* (No. III.); this is inferior to either, but appears to combine characteristics of both. I have discussed it fully in Chapter III. of the *Lancelot* studies, before referred to, and have there compared it with the similar adventure also attributed to that knight in the Dutch compilation.

12. PAGE 61.—*Had it not been for a ring which Lancelot wore.* This is evidently the ring given him by the Lady of the Lake, and referred to in *The Charrette* (ll. 2348 et seq). It had the power of detecting enchantments.

13. PAGE 67.—*King Arthur—held captive the king, who had erst*

*made him a prisoner.* There seems to be a confusion here; from Gariet's account it was the King of the Saxons who captured Arthur; here he has disappeared and everything is attributed to the King of Ireland. Probably they were allies; but it is also possible that confusion may have arisen from the fact that the King of Dublin was at one time, as in the Tristan legend, a Viking, and the poet has not distinguished clearly between the nationalities of these sea-robbers. If so, it would seem to indicate an early date for this particular story.

Made in the USA
Las Vegas, NV
18 October 2022

57714433R00044